Gangway!

M

Donald E. "Westlake" and Brian Garfield

Published by M. Evans and Company, Inc., New York
AND DISTRIBUTED IN ASSOCIATION WITH
J. B. Lippincott, Philadelphia and New York

This is for the boys at the table

1

Gabe had a window seat on the train, but there hadn't been anything to see for three thousand miles.

There had been green days: grass flats, fourteen Indians riding around the train in warbonnets chasing five spavined buffalo. There had been brown days: the occasional yokel on a horse and at intervals an excuse for a town—a few tottering shacks, buckboard wagons, tall idiots festooned with huge revolvers and silly hats.

He remembered the curl of Twill's lip. "West of the Hudson River it's all horse manure."

A wise observation, that. It even smelled that way—even Chicago. Especially Chicago, stinking to high heaven of beef carcasses. It was only a thousand miles after Chicago that you started to remember the place with a certain wistful fondness: It wasn't a city, but at least by God it was trying.

Twill, he thought. He remembered the great big grin on Twill's fat face. Twill had painted a big white X across Gabe's back and then sunk the knife and twisted it. "Would you be showin' the lad out of town, bies?"

This misbegotten wilderness.

Twill would get his. Gabe brooded at the plush seatback in front of him and plotted his triumphal return to Hell's Kitchen. Someday soon. Someday. . . .

A thousand miles of no shade but your own shadow. Five hundred miles crawling upgrade and down, trestles shuddering under the weight of the train, not even a decent paving stone to look at anywhere.

Was the train slowing?

He couldn't see any excuse for it. A lot of muddy hills. *Muddy* hills: the train passed a prospector who either had very short legs or was standing in mud up to his knees.

A few shacks now. Magnificent architectural style they had out here in the West: everything was brand new, but it all looked a hundred years old, fifty years abandoned, and ready to fall over with the next breeze.

But the train was definitely slowing.

Through the filthy pane he saw trees go by, then more shacks, then something with a false front and big weathered lettering: SALOON in a crescent across the boards. Horses standing hipshot in front of it, swishing their tails and stomping the mud.

The train was behaving exactly as though it was going to stop. And the other passengers were getting to their feet. Collecting carpetbags and valises, crowding toward the vestibules.

Gabe pulled out his golden snap-lid pocket timepiece. Half past nine in the morning. A week ago at this time he'd have been making the collection rounds on Tenth Avenue. Towing a couple of guys along with him to beat up on the reluctant ones. He wondered who was doing the collections now.

He clicked the watch shut. Engraved on the case was the legend *For G.B. from P.T. 1873*. He wondered if Twill knew he still had the watch. Probably Twill had forgotten it—

otherwise he'd have told the "bies" to relieve Gabe of it before they hustled him onto the train with the one-way ticket to oblivion and the mild parting words: "Mister Twill says it might not be too brilliant if you ever decided to come back here. You just keep going west until your hat floats, Mister Twill says."

Mister Twill's turn would come.

A lot of beat-up buildings now. Brisk traffic of horses and hicks, a lot of them stopping to watch the train, gawking as if it was the most exciting thing they'd ever seen. Gabe rolled his eyes upward in disbelieving disgust.

Could this be the Coast? The train was lurching past buildings and through the alleys he glimpsed trees and the glint of water.

Water. He shuddered.

"Mind if I sit here?"

He glanced up and around. It was a stout citizen laden with bundles and a big round smile. Everybody else was standing up, this guy wanted to sit down.

Gabe shrugged; the stout man fell into the seat like a bed falling out a window. A duffelbag bounced off Gabe's elbow and he shoved it back into the stout citizen's lap.

He didn't seem to mind. "I always walk to the front of the train," he said cheerfully. "I just don't know why I do that."

"I don't either," Gabe said. He looked out the window. A platform, a lot of rail sidings. They were arriving somewhere, all right.

The conductor came through, bawling, "Endathaline. Endathaline."

End of the line. In more ways than one. Gabe stared mournfully through the pane, his eyes full of memories of Manhattan. "So this is San Francisco," he said.

"No."

"No?"

"This is Sacramento," the stout man said.

Gabe turned around to look at him. "Who?"

"Sacramento. The railroad stops here. It's a hundred miles from here to San Francisco. They haven't finished that part yet."

"The train's supposed to be coast to coast. They said coast to coast." Gabe heard his voice rising, but he didn't care. "A hundred miles more through that *mud*? On *foot*?"

"Not at all, not at all. You see that wharf over there?"

It was sliding gently past. A short pier attached to a long paddlewheel boat. He'd seen boats like that on the Hudson all the time—they plied up and down to Albany. The boat was all gingerbread and brightwork. People were streaming up the gangplanks onto several decks.

The stout man said, "You take that riverboat if you want to get to San Francisco."

"It's not fair," Gabe muttered.

"Why? What's the matter?"

He remembered Twill, acidly polite: *Now you got your choice, Gabe me bie. You can have the train or you can have a lovely sea voyage round the Horn. Just so long as you don't get off till you've reached San Francisco. Now am I not bein' fair, bie? You can't be sayin' old Patrick Twill was after bein' ungenerous to you.*

Why San Francisco? Because Twill had an associate in San Francisco who would be advised to keep an eye on Gabe. *You see, bie, if you don't show up, why we'll just be obliged to issue a sort of warrant for you.*

Well, Twill had issued warrants before, and Gabe himself had carried some of them out—generally in brass but sometimes in lead.

Knowing Twill's mind, Gabe had pleaded and begged to be allowed to go on the boat. He just loved ocean voyages, he said. He hated trains. If God meant us to ride on sooty contraptions like that He'd never have invented the stage-coach.

Gabe had been very convincing. He'd had to be; it was a matter of life and death. He had to persuade Twill that he hated trains, because it was the only way to insure that Twill would put him on a train. Good Christ, just the *thought* of a boat. . . .

"Pardon me," the stout man murmured. He looked genu-inely concerned. "Aren't you well?"

Gabe didn't answer. The train was lurching to a halt with a shriek of scraping brake shoes, and he still had his neck craned around to stare at the gaudy riverboat. He didn't quite feel up to opening his mouth.

"You really don't look fit at all," the stout man said.

Gabe essayed a shrug. He still didn't look around.

Then he felt the touch of the pudgy hand on his arm. "I think I understand," the stout man said, soothingly. "A touch of *mal de mer*, is it?"

"Ung?"

"Yes, that's definitely it. You're susceptible to the malaise of the sea, I judge."

"Ung?"

"You get seasick, don't you?"

Gabe lifted his shoulders as though to dismiss this thrust.

"Well I shouldn't worry if I were you," the stout man said, briskly. "It's only a river, you know. No waves, no pitching or rolling. It's quite a smooth journey, I assure you. No rougher than this train."

"Urp."

"No really, I promise you. Surely you don't get seasick on rivers!"

Gabe finally looked at him. He didn't have to say anything.

The stout man scrutinized Gabe's face and turned both fat palms up. "On rivers?"

"On rainy days!"

"My," the stout man murmured. "That *is* a shame." He shook his head in sympathy.

He turned his back again and stared at the motionless panorama of Sacramento until he heard the stout man begin to stir and rustle. A lot of stirring and rustling—gathering up all the bundles probably. Finally his voice, from slightly up above, rolled against the back of Gabe's head:

"Well I do hope you don't have too bad a time of it."

Gabe nodded without turning. He saw people leaving the train and accosting porters. Most of them headed across the platform toward the riverboat wharf.

At last he turned and looked through the coach. The stout man was gone and so was everybody else.

Reluctantly Gabe got to his feet and dragged them down the aisle to the vestibule.

A porter waited at the foot of the steps but Gabe shook his head, dropped to the platform, and caught a tail-of-the-eye glimpse of the porter's disapproving look. Gabe had no luggage. He had nothing at all, in fact, but the clothes on his back: a cheap pinstripe suit and a cloth cap with a stubby visor. His pockets were stuffed with oddments that made them bulge here and there; he could have brought a knapsack but he had never owned one. Never had reason to. He had been born in Hell's Kitchen twenty-eight years ago and until he'd boarded this train he'd never been west of Twelfth Avenue. Which had been far enough for him. Because if you wanted to get off Manhattan Island, you had to cross water. Obviously that was impossible. Fortunately they'd built the railroad bridge last year, so he hadn't had to start this journey on the ferryboat.

It wasn't just his aversion to water. He'd liked it in Hell's

Kitchen. He practically owned Hell's Kitchen. Well, Twill practically owned it, but Gabe had been Twill's right-hand man because Twill was shanty-Irish and Hell's Kitchen was a tough French slum. If you wanted things smooth you had to have a French right hand. Gabe—Gabriel Beauchamps— came from an impeccable lineage, a dynasty of Marseille thugs. Even the Corsicans in Hell's Kitchen respected the name Beauchamps as long as you pronounced it right. None of this silly *Beechum* business. It was *Bo-champs*, and Gabe had skinned a few knuckles teaching that to a few ignorant toughs.

It had been a good life. But into every life a little brick must fall. Now in the summer of 1874 Gabe found himself at the wrong end of five days on the transcontinental railroad. Five days and three thousand miles and he still hadn't seen anything he'd call a city. A lot of these burgs didn't even have gaslights.

He'd be back. He'd be back to take the Big Apple away from Twill and send *Twill* on a nice sea journey. But to do that he needed cash, plenty of cash. Enough to buy off Twill's protectors.

Cash. If San Francisco turned out to be another of those clapboard-and-mud Chump Junctions like the ones the train had been rolling through these last five days, Gabe just didn't know what he was going to do. . . .

A little blackboard hung beside the ticket window on the wharf. *Steamer New World—Next Sailing* 11:00 A.M. Gabe pulled out the engraved gold watch. Ten forty-five.

He sidled up to the window. "Look, uh——"

"What you want?" The clerk was bored, hung over, or both.

"Look, there's got to be some other way to get to San Francisco."

The bloodshot eyes flicked at him. "Maybe is. But you don't look like Jesus Christ to me."

"Huh?"

"You'd have to walk across San Francisco Bay. Of course you could go around. There's freight wagons go around the Bay. Sometimes they take passengers."

"How long does that take?"

"Eight days, maybe ten. Depends on the weather. You might find one over the other side of the railroad yards. How much money you got?"

"Why?"

"Those muleskinners charge high for passengers. They don't like being crowded on the high seat. You got to pay if you want a ride."

"How much?"

"I ain't sure what it's at this week. Last week they were getting two hundred bucks. In gold, not paper."

"Two hundred bucks?"

"Aeah. Of course you could always walk. Only take you a month or so."

Gabe looked down at his shoes. The soles needed repairing right now. One day's hiking, let alone a month's. . . .

"I've got to think on this." He swung away.

The clerk's voice followed him cheerily. "Think quick, friend. *New World* sets off in ten minutes, and she's always on time, she is. Next boat ain't till tomorrow this time and you don't. . . ."

Whatever it was the clerk had to say, Gabe didn't catch the rest. He was suddenly very busy avoiding being trampled.

It was a small wagon. Small but drawn by ten teams of mules. Each mule seemed to have forty hoofs. Clots of mud ricocheted off the ticket office and off Gabe's suit. There was a great swell and rush of movement, and the wagon went caroming by him as if it had a boat to catch.

· *14* ·

It was all noise and wheeling confusion but as Gabe leaped back his eyes whipped across the words YANKEE BAR MINE painted on the side of the wagon. He tumbled back against the ticket window and gathered breath to yell something unfriendly, but the remark died on his lips.

What curbed his tongue was the size of the ten horsemen escorting the little wagon.

They were armed to the teeth and they looked like boulders hewn out of granite mountains. They all had expressions like closed doors. Rifles and shotguns in their fists, great spurs on their boots, revolver handles sprouting from their waists like weed crops.

The horsemen went thundering by like agents of the Apocalypse. While Gabe got his balance and started to dust himself off—*mud myself off?*—the whole army came to a swirling halt around the wagon at the end of the wharf, at the foot of the wide freight gangplank.

The big guys on horseback made a tight circle around the wagon, facing outward with rifles and shotguns propped against their thighs. They all kept looking around in all directions as though they'd just received word that something fun to shoot was about to appear.

Anything guarded that zealously deserved Gabe's attention. He moved that way, easing past various wagons, stevedores and spectators. Beyond the wharf the river cut through town and disappeared into a valley of trees and mud. Little boats churned up and downstream. It was all busy and noisy under the August sun.

Half the horsemen were dismounting now. The rest appeared to grow larger to fill the gaps. The guys on foot slung their rifles over their shoulders and began to unload small wooden boxes from the wagon. The boxes were no bigger than shoes but the big guys were lifting only one apiece. It was clear from all the grunting and heaving that they were not filled with gossamer and lace. Gabe drifted closer for a better look. Immediately two of the mounted guards fixed their glares on him with obvious and belligerent expectation of trouble.

Gabe smiled disarmingly and took another step.

The nearest guard's flinty stare drilled into him, but then it slid away without change of expression. Obviously he didn't consider Gabe a threat. A dude, and alone.

It irritated Gabe to be dismissed lightly. But on the other hand it might not be bright to change the guard's opinion right now. Gabe rose above injured pride—and moved a step closer to the wagon.

The boxes were moving up the gangplank, one by one. He watched a guard pick up one of them from the wagon. Made of rough wood, the box had a tag hanging from it. The tag was stenciled in black:

TO: U. S. MINT, SAN FRANCISCO

"Hey friend."

Gabe looked slowly toward the big guy on the horse.

"Me?"

"You."

"You want something from me?"

"I want you should get back away from that wagon."

"I just wanted to look," Gabe said reasonably. "There's no harm in looking."

"You want to look at that gold," the big guy said, "you can visit it at the Mint."

Gabe looked at the wagon and back up at the big guy. "Thanks," he said. "Maybe I will."

The big guy lowered the muzzle of his rifle an inch. Gabe backed off and made a half turn, back toward the ticket window. That brought the stern of the riverboat into view, past the side of the wharf. The stern was riding slowly up and down. Gabe fixed his eyes on it, mesmerized.

He just didn't like the motion of that boat. Three gang-planks connected it with the pier; passengers and freight were going steadily aboard and the boat was moving softly up and down, up and down, up and down. Not even in a regular motion like the click-click-click of the train wheels, but in a sickening rolling manner that first attracted Gabe's eye, then his mind, and then his stomach. . . .

Oh, no.

He wheeled around and locked his eyes on the first station-ary object: a sign next to the ticket window, which said:

Fares:

Pittsburg	$2
Port Chicago	$4
Richmond	$9
San Francisco	$16.50

Sure, he thought.

The clerk at the window leered at him. "Four minutes, friend."

They had a language of their own out here, and Gabe was beginning to learn the vocabulary. When a guy called you *friend,* it was like when a tiger showed you his teeth. It didn't pay to assume he was smiling.

Over on the wharf the gold wagon was empty and the mule-skinner was bellowing a rich stream of oaths at his animals. The wagon curled away. Four characters in overalls came out of a shed and took the reins of the big guys' horses. All the big guys were dismounted now, half of them up on the forward deck and the other half stomping toward the gangplank.

So the guards were traveling with the gold, not with the wagon. They were all clustering around the pile of gold boxes on deck now and keeping the passengers away.

Passengers. Gabe looked off to his right, and it seemed as though just about everybody who'd been on the train was already on the boat. If he didn't hustle himself, he'd get left behind and not make it to San Francisco. And if there was one thing worse than being on that riverboat it was not being on it, if the alternative was life in this place. What did that fat fellow say it was? Sacramento.

Plus there was Twill, and that associate of Twill's waiting for Gabe to show up in San Francisco. It would be a very very poor idea to disappoint him.

Also, there was that gold. For some reason Gabe liked the idea of traveling with a wagonload of gold for companionship. It made a voyage by boat almost worthwhile.

Almost. Taking a step closer to the ticket window, Gabe gave the sign beside it an affronted look. To hear that sign talk, you'd think California was nothing but major metropolises. Pittsburg, Port Chicago, Richmond indeed. The truth was that these gully-jumpers wouldn't know a city if it fell on them.

The ticket clerk said, "You goin someplace, or you just practicin your lip-readin?"

Gabe lifted one eyebrow in a big-city stare. "You in a hurry?"

"No, I'm not, but you ought to be. The boat's about to leave."

Gabe looked over at the boat, and damn if they weren't starting to pull the gangplanks in. "Yeah," he said. "I'm going to San Francisco."

"You are if you run for it." The clerk slapped a ticket down on the counter. "That'll be sixteen and four bits."

"Ah. Well, I——"

Gabe hadn't known about this extra expense at the end of the line and wasn't sure exactly how much cash he still had. He'd left New York in something of a hurry and hadn't been able to scrounge together too much of a road stake. Did he even *have* sixteen dollars and fifty cents?

He watched the gangplanks sliding upward over there at

the boat while he fumbled in his pockets. A ten-dollar eagle. A five-dollar half eagle.

He dug. He dug fast now because he had sudden thoughts of the telegram that would go out to Twill if Gabe didn't show up in San Francisco. He dug through every pocket and, counting the dime in his left trouser cuff, he had seventeen dollars and five cents.

"There you are," Gabe said at last, dumping a double handful of coins onto the counter.

"And there *you* are," the clerk said. "Have a great trip."

That just had to be sarcastic. Clutching his ticket Gabe peered at the clerk's face, but saw only a guileless smile as the man closed the board shutters over his window.

And a lot of shouting was taking place over at the riverboat. Gabe saw only one gangplank still connecting ship to pier, and he made a run for it, waving the ticket and shouting, "Hi! Hi!"

The scenery was moving. Hills were going by. There was open water between Gabe and the nearest land. And the water was moving and the boat was moving.

Slowly, like a statue toppling off a pedestal, Gabe bent over the rail.

2

She came walking happily along the deck, smiling in the sunshine. It was good to be sailing the Sacramento River once again. I really ought to do it more often, she thought. A change of air, a couple of days in the sun—it could do wonders for a girl's complexion.

She turned into the saloon lounge and cast her eye over the crowd. Pilgrims, most of them. The crowd was denser in the men's bar, but she wasn't allowed in there of course. In the saloon lounge ladies in stays and heavy dresses sat fanning themselves against the heat. Fools—but they'd learn.

She went out again to take a turn on deck; she hadn't explored the port side yet. She knew she was drawing stares from the gentlemen passengers but she didn't acknowledge any of them although she knew how—the droop of an eyelash, the loss of a handkerchief. Today she was not interested in romance.

Toward the bow she turned past the lifeboat and suddenly a huge tough loomed, blocking her way.

"Sorry, Miss. You can't go up no further."

The rifle was large in his fists. His eyes were sizing her up in appreciation.

She blinked at him. "But I always ride up front. I love to ride up front."

"Sorry, Miss. Everybody stays back of this line today."

"Oh," she said. "Another gold shipment."

"Yes, Miss."

"They're such a bore."

She felt the guard's eyes on her when she turned away. She glanced up and saw the Captain on the texas deck. He was watching her, too. It made her smile a little and it put a little extra bounce in her step.

She went through the forward corridor to the starboard side. A few gentlemen stood at the rail. She saw a thin young fellow in an Eastern suit, alone. His face was loose and grey and filled with alarm and unease. His shoes looked a bit worn, and he was clutching a cloth cap in one trembling hand. He looked as if he'd come from way back East somewhere, maybe from as far as St. Louis or Indianapolis. From the condition he was in it appeared he'd had a rough trip.

He might be worth checking out, she thought, but first there were the two prosperous merchants talking business by the davits. She headed sedately in their direction.

3

Gabe clung to the heaving, pitching deck of the boat while it tied up at the dock of Pittsburg.

Pittsburg, he observed without believing. Maybe five buildings and a pier. If you counted a tack shed as a building.

He clutched a passing nautical type by the sleeve. "How long will we be tied up here?"

"Ten minutes. Maybe fifteen."

Gabe rushed to the gangplank and staggered down to the little pier. Got on solid ground and stood there taking deep breaths. His vision began to clear.

He looked up toward the forward deck. The big guys stood like trees. So San Francisco had a U. S. Mint, did it? And gold was shipped there.

That was interesting. Very interesting.

He was still thinking about that when a sailor in a striped shirt went by bawling, "All aboard—all aboard," which suggested these Westerners couldn't tell the difference between a steamboat and a train.

Gabe dragged himself aboard.

He draped himself over the rail as near as he could get to

the gold stack, because he thought maybe if he could keep looking at all that gold it would take his mind off being seasick.

It didn't work out that way. But between spells of being violently sick and spells of dry heaves, there were the occasional merciful moments of respite. During one of those moments he caught sight of a girl drifting unhurriedly along the deck, stopping here and there to look around her with pert wide-eyed interest. A slip of a girl, a delicate innocent flower of a girl. She wasn't looking in his direction; she stopped not too far away, a little beauty of a girl sweetly taking deep breaths of the warm and sunny afternoon air.

The lovely wisp of a girl, wearing chaste innocence like a clean fragrance, moved daintily past Gabe. He would have turned to watch her go, but his time was up. He lurched back over the rail, clutched a stanchion with one hand, and hung his head weakly, keeping his eyes tight shut so he wouldn't have to watch the water roll past below him. Desperately his mind clung to a vision of the girl he had just seen. The simple dainty frock she wore; the wind gently whipping the long blonde hair around her little face . . .

Something jostled him slightly. In his wracked condition, he hardly noticed.

The first he knew anything was wrong was when he heard the shot and the scream.

He whipped around, as fast as he could under the circumstances, and slapped his right hand against his hip pocket where his knuckle-duster was.

Except it wasn't.

He realized the pocket was empty at the same time that he saw the girl. The same girl he'd been dreaming about, trying to distract himself from his stomach. Damn if Gabe's knuckleduster wasn't in her hand, still smoking at the muzzle as she held it out away from her as though it were a dead rat.

"Well, by God," Gabe muttered. He pushed himself away from the rail and reached for his property. "I'll take that."

But she held onto it; partly from panic, it seemed, and partly from a grasping nature. She glared at him, her jaw set, and held on tight.

Gabe felt as weak as railroad beer. He yanked at the knuckle-duster, clutching his cap in his other hand, and panted, "Gimme that. Give it to me."

"No." She said it through clenched teeth and held on.

The knuckle-duster was turning this way and that in their hands, neither of them able to keep a firm grip on it. One of them—probably the girl, who obviously had no idea what it was she'd stolen—accidentally touched the concealed button on the side. The duster's knife-blade snapped open, flipping up between all those fingers without quite removing any of them.

"Sheee!" The girl let go in a sudden hurry and jumped backward.

Gabe slapped his cap on his head to free his other hand, then disengaged the blade and folded it shut. Opening the single-shot chamber, he rummaged in his cluttered pockets for a new cartridge. At the same time he kept one eye on the girl and the other on the corner of the forward cabin beyond which the gold guards were clustered. They weren't visible from here, but it was curious that the sound of the shot hadn't brought them on the run.

No. It wasn't curious after all. They knew their business, those guys. They weren't about to be distracted from the gold by some trivial diversion like a gunshot sounding within forty feet of them.

He found a .41 cartridge and thumbed it into the knuckle-duster in the chamber between the brass knuckles and the knife. Then he shoved the weapon back in his hip pocket where it belonged and took two steps backward to bring the gold stack in view.

The guards down there were all staring in his direction, and now when he came in sight they all took fresh grips on their shotguns and stared at him a little harder.

The girl had recovered fast. Indignant, she demanded, "What sort of thing *is* that?"

Gabe moved back into the shadow, out of the gold guards' line of sight—and fire. "None of your business," he muttered.

The girl was rubbing her knuckles and frowning like a folded-up awning. "Mister," she said, "there ought to be a law against you."

He stared at her. "Against *me!*"

"Going around with that—*thing* in your pocket. You could hurt some——"

"Now just wait one minute!"

"——body." She stamped a little foot. "You've got no right to carry a thing like that in a pocket where you ought to be carrying your wallet. And furthermore——"

"And furthermore," he said, leaning close over her to drown her out, "I'm thinking I ought to turn you in to the captain for picking pockets."

The girl opened her mouth, but this time didn't manage to say anything. Gabe glanced toward the cabin corner to see if any of the gold guards planned to mosey on down this way. None were in sight, but at that moment a wide man with a rolling gait and an official-looking cap came swinging around the corner instead. He came bearing down on them like an express wagon. "I heard a shot."

Gabe glanced at the girl. Her eyes were very round and large.

Gabe shrugged. "We didn't hear anything." He tipped his head toward the girl. "You hear anything?"

"No. Not a thing."

"I didn't either," Gabe said. "A shot, you say?"

"Sounded like a pistol to me," the wide man said suspiciously. His nostrils were wrinkling. "I could swear I smell powdersmoke."

"I don't smell a thing," the girl said.

The wide man stood with his shoes planted three feet apart and scratched his head in bafflement. The girl moved closer to him, looked up into his downcast face, and then reached up and thumbed one of his eyelids back. "You sure you're feeling all right?"

The wide man jerked his head back. "I feel fine. What are you talking about?"

"Maybe a touch too much sun," the girl said, mostly to herself. "I'd stay under cover for a while if I were you. Do you hear things very often? Smell things?"

"I—uh——"

"I'm a nurse, you see. I've seen cases before."

"Cases? Cases of what?"

She had the wide guy worried now. But she only smiled sweetly. "It's nothing to worry about, I promise you. A little too much sun can do it, you know. Take my advice, Captain, stay out of the——"

"I ain't the Captain. I'm the Mate."

"All right, Mate. Stay out of the sun for a day or two. That's my advice." The girl turned smartly, hooked her arm in the bend of Gabe's elbow, and promenaded aft with him along the deck.

Near the stern Gabe stopped and shook her arm off. Up forward the Mate was still scratching his head, but presently he put his cap back on and his wide shape rolled into the corridor doorway and disappeared.

"Nurse," Gabe snorted.

"Thanks for not turning me in." She was doing her demure-little-girl act again. So sweet, so pretty. Sweet as laudanum poison, he thought.

But she was pretty all right.

Frowning, which didn't spoil her prettiness at all, she said, "What *was* that horrible thing anyway?"

"What thing? Oh you mean my knuckle-duster." He looked around—they had no witnesses. So he took it out of his pocket and slipped the brass rings over his fingers and showed her. "Like that. See, you can hit him with it. Or you can cut him with it. Or if you're really mad you can shoot him."

Wide-eyed, she looked at him in wonder mixed with doubt. "What sort of a person," she said, "would carry a thing like that?"

Feeling pretty expansive, Gabe stowed the knuckle-duster away in its pocket again and said, "Well, I'm from New York, see. Back there, you know, men are men, and you got to be prepared to defend yourself. Not like these joskins out here."

She glared. "Out where?"

"Out here in the hicks."

She took a deep breath and her lips pinched into a thin line. "I guess," she said coldly, "you mustn't ever have been to San Francisco."

"Sweetheart, I haven't seen anything you could call a city since I stepped on the train in Manhattan, and I don't have very high hopes for San Francisco."

"San Francisco," she said, standing up very straight, "is the Paris of the West."

"Well, that's real nice," Gabe said. "New York isn't the Paris of anyplace. It's the New York of the world, the only one, and all I want from my life is to get back to it."

The angrier she got, the taller she wanted to be. She was now up on the balls of her feet, teetering there like a beer bottle when you thump your fist on the table. "If New York is so wonderful," she demanded, "why'd you leave it?"

It's not as if I had a choice, he thought. But what he said was, "Well—a man's got to see the world. How'd I have known New York was the only place in the world worth being in if I never went anywhere else?"

"That's not true."

"What do you mean it's not true? I haven't seen a single——"

"That's not what I mean. You're not telling me the whole story."

"What whole story?"

"Hah," she said in disgust. "Here you are three thousand miles from home with that—knuckle-duster thing in your pocket, and no money, and a tough line of——"

"What do you mean no money?"

"Brother, I went through your pockets like a squirrel through a bag of peanuts. I can tell you what color lint you're carrying around. And you haven't got a cent in your kick. Well, to be exact, you haven't got a cent in your kick *now*."

He jammed his hand into his trouser pocket where he'd put the change after he'd bought the boat ticket.

Nothing.

"You used to have fifty-five cents," she told him sweetly.

Gabe peeled his lips back from his teeth. "Give—it—back."

"Fifty-five cents." She made a face, produced the six coins from the enormous bag she had slung over her shoulder, and dropped the money coin by coin into his open palm. "There you are my good man."

"Of all the——"

"Now you've got fifty-five cents. But I'd still call that no money."

"Maybe my money's waiting for me in San Francisco."

She grinned. "So's mine," she said. "In somebody else's pocket. Exactly the same as you."

"A pickpocket calling *me* a crook. I've heard a lot of——"

"Oh come *on*. You didn't turn me in."

"I should have. I still should." But he felt he was losing control of the conversation, and it irritated him.

"But you didn't and you won't. Because you don't want to talk to the police any more than I do."

He said truculently, "I'm not wanted anywhere."

"I can well believe that."

"The only reason I didn't turn you in was because——" He stopped abruptly. It wasn't true anyway. There were *two* reasons. One, he'd never turned anybody in to the law; it was against his philosophy. And two, she was too pretty to turn in. But he was damned if he was going to tell her that out loud.

Besides, his stomach suddenly reminded him he was on a boat.

"Because what?" she challenged.

"Never mind."

"You're turning a little green. Don't tell me you're going to be sick again."

"Shut up."

"You've already thrown up everything you've had to eat for the past six months. How can you have anything left to throw up?"

"Urp. . . ."

He knew the riverboat was slowing again because he could feel the alteration of its motion in the pit of his stomach. He swallowed painfully and lifted his head to look toward shore. "What the hell is that?"

"Port Chicago."

Four buildings and a pier. "Chicago."

"*Port* Chicago. There's a difference."

"I can see there is." Gabe's eyes rolled upward, seeking inspiration from the sky. "Pittsburg was bigger than this!"

"Wait till you see Richmond."

"What's San Francisco? Two stovepipes and a tent?"

4

She found herself liking this self-proclaimed city slicker. It was hard to tell why. He didn't have any money. He didn't like California. He thought everybody who didn't have an accent like his was a hick. She had met plenty of snob dudes with their Boston drawls and their noses in the air, but this one wasn't like that—he was even worse.

She looked at him fondly. He was drooping over the rail in terminal agony and somehow he made her feel protective. Maybe it was because he talked so tough and blustered so much. Her father had been just like that. Underneath he'd been a lamb.

This one was more likely goat than lamb, but there was something appealing in the brave helplessness with which he regarded the world from behind his soulful eyes. He looked underfed and rumpled. His face was an uneven triangle, he tended to talk out of the side of his mouth, he had a voice like lumps of coal rattling down a sheet-metal chute, he wasn't what anybody in the world could possibly call handsome, he was feisty and opinionated—you might even say he was disagreeable; but then you could say all that about a Siamese cat and she loved Siamese cats.

She said, "That's Richmond."

He lifted his head, which had been hanging over the rail. He had a look. "It would be," he said and let his head droop again.

The boat eased up against the rickety pier. Its every shift was echoed by a muffled groan from the dude draped on the rail. Finally the boat stopped, and the dude made a dash for the pier.

She went along with him. "Don't you ever get used to it?"

"To tell you the truth," he said glumly, "I haven't gone out of my way to try."

The midafternoon sun was warm on deck. She waited for him to come up from the rail to the nearly vertical. He kept hold on the rail, but it was one of his respite periods between relapses. She was learning to time his cycles and she didn't bother to talk to him except during the respites.

"Maybe we ought to introduce ourselves," she said. "What do you call yourself?"

"Unless I want me, I don't call."

"Well, my name's Evangeline."

"Evangeline," he said in a flat tone of voice, looking at her with an expression that implied he didn't believe a bit of it but that it didn't surprise him because it wasn't the first time he'd been lied to.

"That's the truth. Evangeline Kemp."

"Sure."

"No, really."

He looked her over. "Your parents sure didn't know much when they named you."

"You bite your tongue!"

"I only speak as a gent whose pocket you picked. What do folks call you? Vangie?"

"Not if they care whether I speak to them or not. My name is Evangeline. E–van–ge–line."

"Well, I'll tell you, Vangie," he said weakly. "Right now four syllables is more than I can handle all at once."

"I'd rather be called Hey-You."

"In your line of work you probably are, most of the time."

"That was the first time in my life I ever did anything like that," she said.

He just looked at her.

She shifted around a bit, looking defensive. "That's the truth," she said.

"Fine," he said. "Now tell me a lie. I want to see the difference."

"No, really." She leaned toward him, her expression earnest and brave but tragic. "My folks are down in San Francisco," she said, "and all my money was stolen from me, and——"

"Vangie," he said. "Just pretend you told me the whole story, all right?"

Innocent bewilderment spread across her face. "Story?"

"Let's just say," he suggested, "that I'm not quite as gullible as some of these acorn-crackers you're used to around here."

She would have had a comment on that, but he'd hardly got the statement out before he was into another relapse. Evangeline left him in disgust and took a turn around the deck. When she returned he was still draped over the rail with one eye on the big toughs who stood in a circle around the stack of gold boxes.

He looked like a consumptive with the wadded handkerchief pressed against his mouth, but she knew that wasn't it. She'd never seen such a persistent case of seasickness before.

It was a terrible thing. She patted his shoulder. "I'm sorry. Really."

He looked at her balefully, but when the relapse ended he straightened up and said, "It's supposed to be funny."

"I don't think it's funny."

"You don't, do you," he said. He was looking at her in a different way now.

"Well it must be very painful. I mean I don't see anything to laugh about."

"That's real sweet of you, Vangie."

"You'll feel better when we get to dry land."

"Yeah."

Liking him, feeling a strange sort of comradeship, a kind of rapport, she said, "You still haven't told me your name."

"Uh," he said. He looked pale, but alert. "It's, uh, John Lexington."

So much for rapport. "What do people mostly call you?" she asked. "Mister Avenue?"

It was his turn to display injured innocence. "What's *that* supposed to mean?"

"I maybe never was *in* New York City," she said, "but I've *heard* of it. And I've heard of Lexington Avenue."

"Well, it's a name," he said. "They called it after somebody, didn't they?"

"Not after you. Come on, now, I told you my real name."

"E–van–ge–line Kemp," he said slowly, working the name over like a tough steak. "Yeah, you probably did."

"I did."

"Mine's Gabe," he said.

"Gabe what?"

"Beauchamps."

"Bo-champs?"

"Right."

"What's the Gabe stand for?"

"Gabe," he said. "Excuse me."

She watched him go into another relapse, sagging over the rail once more like a mattress hanging out a window to air. She studied him with a mixture of sympathy and awe. "Don't you ever empty?"

"Uuuurrrrg."

5

Gabe watched the water go by. How could there be so much water in the world?

"There it is," the girl said.

He went on peering droop-lidded at the water. Whatever it was, he didn't see it. "Where?"

"Not down there. Over there. San Francisco!" She made it sound like a fanfare of cornets.

He lifted his head—it weighed a ton—and saw one of the world's biggest small towns. "Oh, that's fine," he said. "That's just dandy."

"We've got tall buildings and everything," she said, on the defensive again.

"You do not. You have short buildings on tall hills. There's a difference."

"We've even got a cable car."

"A what?"

"Never mind. You'll see."

If he lived that long. He collapsed over the rail, wishing he were dead.

But he still had one eye on that gold shipment to the Mint.

The riverboat docked, not without much wrenching and heaving. At long last, clutching Vangie's arm Gabe tottered ashore.

"There now," she said. "Isn't it better to be on dry land?"

Dry land. He lifted one foot and studied his shoe with disapproval. "In New York," he said, "we think of mud as something we like to get rid of."

It made her angry again. "You should just have stayed in New York," she told him.

Gabe looked around. "I know I should have."

It was bleak to look at. From Chicago west the climate had at least been sunny. Sunny all the way to Sacramento and even sunny on the riverboat. But here the clouds seemed to be attached to the tops of the hills. Everything was grey and dreary. It matched Gabe's mood. Fifty-five cents in his pocket and nobody waiting to meet him except some "associate" of Twill's. You could bet there wouldn't be any help forthcoming from that quarter.

The passengers had gathered their luggage and there was a stream of people moving past Gabe and the girl and on in toward town. Hansoms and victorias were drawn up to meet the more important arrivals. The waterfront streets were jammed with a triffic of pedestrians, horses and wagons. Narrow streets, he noted with approval. Almost narrow enough to qualify as city streets. At least they weren't like those half-mile-wide flats of rutted dust that passed for streets in the towns he'd passed through the past five days.

It was about six o'clock and the sun would be up for another two or three hours, which didn't matter much because the clouds blotted it out completely, obscuring the tops of the hills and sending wispy tendrils down toward the Bay. Gaslights and oil lamps were lit everywhere along the streets. It was freezing goddam cold for August.

Horse-drawn trolleys clanged past along the waterfront and

there was a swaggering mass to the crowd that shifted like heavy liquid through the alleys, streets and piers. Forty or fifty ships were lined up along the Bay shore, smokestacks and masts making a forest along the docks; there was a great deal of racket. It wasn't busy enough or loud enough to make him feel at home, but at least it wasn't quite as bad as what he'd been braced to find here.

He began to look at faces. He had no way of knowing who Twill's associate was but, if it was somebody Twill knew well enough to trust, it might just be somebody recognizable. Not that Gabe expected to recognize him as an individual, but he might spot the type. You didn't see many Hell's Kitchen mugs around here.

But there were too many faces flowing past. None of them drew his attention. Was Twill's man somewhere in the crowd, just watching? There was no reason to expect the man to make himself known. Then again there was no reason not to. The guy might very well come up to Gabe and drop a few words of warning.

But nobody did.

Vangie was starting off. "Well? You coming?"

"Just a minute." He turned and looked back down the pier toward the riverboat. He hated the riverboat so that wasn't what he was looking at; if he never saw the *New World* again it would be far too soon.

What he was interested in was the gold. The big guys were unloading it from the deck. There was a wagon drawn up by the freight gangplank and he could read its sign from here: UNITED STATES MINT. Half a dozen horseback guards. The big guys were bringing the stuff down a box at a time, the same way they'd done the reverse in Sacramento. As the pile on deck diminished and the pile in the wagon grew, the number of big guys with each pile shifted accordingly. In the end almost all the big guys were on the dock, standing in a circle around the wagon, shoulder to shoulder, rifles ready for the Battle of Gettysburg.

He turned back to Vangie at last and asked half absent-mindedly, "Where is this Mint anyway?"

She pointed up the nearest hill. "Up there."

It was at the very top, shrouded in the mist that hung from the underbellies of the clouds. But up there along the incredibly steep cobblestoned street, past many blocks of stores and saloons and houses and hotels, he had a vague grey picture of a huge forbidding fortress, a structure of stone-block and iron gates and castle turrets like the Manhattan Armory.

He must have grunted because Vangie said, "What about it?"

"Just interested."

"You wouldn't be thinking about trying to steal one of those gold shipments, would you?"

"I wouldn't dream of that."

"That's good. Just take another look at those toughs and their rifles."

It wasn't hard to take another look at them. It would have been harder not to, since the gold wagon and its escort were at that moment rumbling right past them. Mounts had been brought for the big guys, and they were twice as big on horseback as they had been before. One of them—the guy Gabe had talked to in Sacramento—gave Gabe a quick cold glance as he rode by. The mud flew, the wagon rattled and the hoofs thundered. The wagon this time was drawn by at least twenty teams, and it was easy to see why: If that high hill had been any steeper it would have been a cliff.

Vangie had been watching him while he'd been watching the gold, and now she said, "And don't think about trying to break into the Mint."

"Mmm?"

"It can't be done."

"You mean nobody's done it."

"I mean it can't be done." She turned. "Come on, will you?"

"Where?"

"My belly feels like my throat's been cut. And as for you —you've just *got* to be hungry after all the food you left in the Sacramento River."

"Now that you mention it. . . ."

They moved into a narrow street, getting jostled. Something like grey smoke began to drift down off the rooftops, obscuring their view of things. "What's going on? Something on fire?"

"Shh!" Vangie clapped a finger to Gabe's mouth. "Don't say fire around here. Ever. Unless you mean it."

"But that stuff——"

"That's just the fog coming in."

It was coming in mighty fast. He could hardly see the end of the street, only a block away. "This happen often?"

Defensively she said, "From time to time."

"What's that mean?"

"Well," she said reluctantly, "maybe once or twice a day."

"A *day?*"

"We don't mind it."

"*Every* day?"

"You get used to it."

"All year round?"

She said desperately, "We *like* the fog."

"All right then, tell me this. Does it ever get any warmer around here?"

"Once in a while. From time to time."

"You mean once or twice a day?"

"Well, maybe once or twice a year." She added quickly, "But it never gets much colder than this either."

"I don't see how it hardly could." He shook his head. "And you call this a city."

Just the same at least there was life teeming around them. The narrow street was overflowing with toughs, brassy girls and drunken sailors. Among the buildings Gabe could see, two out of three were Melodeons and Saloons. The rest were whorehouses, opium dens, Cheap John clothing stores, ship-chandlers and the kind of boardinghouses where you kept your boots on when you went to bed to make sure nobody stole them. It was a neighborhood not altogether unlike Hell's Kitchen; even if it was a pretty limp imitation, it did show some promise.

You didn't even have to guess at what the shadier emporiums were. They all had frank signs. *Ye Olde Whore Shoppe. Ye Blinde Pigge.* They didn't leave a whole lot to the imagination. Or maybe they did: It was doubtful most of the passersby could read.

Vangie was leading him around another corner, and Gabe was damned if she wasn't leading him right back down to the docks. "*Now* what?"

"I've just got something to take care of, over on the next pier."

"Take care of what?" But he trailed along onto the pier, and he saw through the descending mist a variety of gaudily painted signs announcing that ships left this spot for such destinations as Alaska, San Pedro, Panama, and New York.

An oceangoing paddlewheel steam packet was tied up at the berth. For a panic-stricken moment Gabe was terrified that Vangie was going to lead him straight on board the damn thing. But she stopped just inside the pier entrance and leaned down to lift the lid of a wooden box. Evidently it had been nailed into place on the boarding.

The box was a cube about a foot in every dimension. There was a slot in its lid, like a ticket-taker's box, and on a stake above the box was a prettily lettered sign:

DID YOU FORGET

From her enormous shoulderbag Vangie took a small key.
It unlocked the padlock on the key box. She lifted the lid
and removed the three keys that reposed in the box. Each key
was attached to a wooden tag bearing the name of a hotel and
a room number.

She closed the box and locked it, putting the three wood-
tagged keys into her bag. "Okay, we can go now."

Gabe walked back up the street with her. "The San Francisco Hotel Association," he said. "*You're* the San Francisco
Hotel Association."

"Well you know lodgings are terribly expensive."

"Uh-huh. And your parents live in San Francisco, and
someone stole all your money, and you were stranded up the
river, and you'd never ever picked anybody's pocket before,
ever."

Vangie shrugged evasively and went on up the street with
a cheerful grin. Her body swung alertly and the huge pocket-
book flew from her little shoulder.

She was *damned* pretty. Gabe found himself thinking it
might be fun to show her around New York. She'd probably
fit right in back there, which was something he hadn't expected from any Westerner.

She paused to look back at him. "You coming?"

"Oh, yes," he said. "I'm coming."

He caught up with her and this time they walked directly
into the city. They passed a Melodeon on a corner. Someone
had splashed a huge X of red paint across its lurid poster of
cancan dancers, and hung on the door a wooden shingle with
CLOSED painted on it in the same vivid red paint.

The sign on the corner was wreathed in fog but there was a gas streetlamp next to it and Gabe could make out the printing. It seemed very important to know that they were at the intersection of Sansome and Pacific Streets. Not that Gabe would ever find it again without a guide. But he liked to know the names of places where there might be opportunities. And Pacific Street looked like such a place. Jammed from sidewalk to sidewalk with moving bodies, most of them unsteady on their feet. And it wasn't even sunset yet.

"Pacific Street," he murmured.

"We call it the Barbary Coast."

"Is that right. What's that mean?"

"I don't know. But I heard a politician say it's the most vice-infested square mile of corruption in the world." She said it with a note of triumph which Gabe didn't miss; suddenly she turned and jabbed a pretty little finger into his chest. "Nobody's ever said that about New York. Hah!"

"Only because New York's bigger than a square mile. We like to spread the joy around a little."

"Oh you're so smart." She lifted her chin and swung away toward a side street.

"Where you going?" He had an instant's panic.

"You wait there," she said.

"For what?"

"Don't you want dinner?"

"We both know my stomach's empty."

"Well, we won't get much for fifty-five cents."

"You mean I'm the only one you hit on that boat?"

She frowned for a moment. "I guess you must have distracted me. But anyway, you wait right here. I'll be back."

And she drifted away into the crowd.

It wouldn't do, he thought. He wasn't going to have a wisp of a girl picking pockets to feed him. It might be standard behavior out here, but back East where men were men. . . .

Pacific Street ran down from where Gabe stood to a flight

of slippery stone steps that gave onto a crude little pier. Both sides of the street were lined with casinos, grog shops, whorehouses and a variety of dives the nature of which was fairly easy to ascertain from a quick study of the people emerging from them. The opium dens were particularly easy to spot that way. Nearby he spotted a Melodeon with a huge poster, eight feet square, the better to illustrate the full proportions of the two very fat lady dancers whose forms were artistically painted above the words THE GALLOPING COW and THE DANCING HEIFER. The whole of it, like the other signs he'd seen, was X-ed out with a huge slash of red paint. Why were all the dance halls closed? It could hardly be for lack of potential business, he observed; the street was teeming with drunks just begging to be separated from their money.

The smells were thick and multifarious, the noise close to earsplitting. It was hard to stand in one place without being whacked and jostled; Gabe faded back against the face of MME. HERZ'S CLOTHING EMPORIUM, which was possibly the most disreputable Cheap John shop he had ever seen.

He remembered briefly the panic that had jabbed him when he'd thought, for an instant there, that Vangie was just going to turn away and leave him in the street. What a ridiculous way for a full grown man to behave. But still, it was the first time in his memory that he'd been in a city where he didn't know every alley and every doorway.

City? Not really. *I mean look at these buildings.* Not a substantial-looking structure in the lot. Everything was wood-frame; it had all been built in a hurry out of green lumber. Everything was splintered, warped, the paint weathered. A sulfur match and one good breeze and the whole thing would go up in smoke.

Was that why she'd got so upset when he'd mentioned fire?

His speculations were interrupted by the arrival of two

burly guys who came meandering along, glanced at him, stopped to give him a second look, went past him, stopped to give him a third look, turned around, came back to him, and eyed him up and down.

One of them licked a thick avaricious lip and said, "Howdy there."

"Hi."

"You lost, friend?"

Right there he knew it was time to get alert. He pushed his shoulder away from the wall so he could stand up straight; he spread his feet a little and gave himself maneuvering room. "No. I'm just waiting for somebody."

"That so," one of the burly guys said. "You're from the East, huh?"

"Damn right I am."

The two guys were starting to move around. One of them sort of turned left, and the other sort of turned right. Like the revolving wooden ducks he'd seen in shooting galleries. They kept shifting, and Gabe had to keep moving around too because otherwise one of them would have got behind him.

"Just get to town, did you?"

"Aeah."

You learned in Hell's Kitchen not to let a stranger get around behind you. You learned that right away, by the age of five, because if you didn't there wasn't too much chance you'd see the age of six. But also there was the matter of being polite. You should face the person you're talking to.

"Well what do you think of our fair city, friend?"

"It's all right," he said without much enthusiasm as they figure-eighted around the sidewalk.

"All kinds of interesting things to see in Frisco," one of the burly guys said.

"All kinds," the other burly guy murmured. His teeth flashed in what he evidently thought was a friendly grin. Gabe had seen some of Twill's toughs grin like that.

Maybe that was it. Twill's associate? Nobody had said anything about *two* associates. But that didn't mean anything. An associate could have an associate, couldn't he?

"Look, are you guys looking for somebody in particular?"

They both stopped figure-eighting around him long enough to look at each other and then look back at Gabe. "Huh?"

"Sorry. My mistake maybe."

The two guys were a little confused but they regained their footwork quick enough. One of them said, "Listen, there's lots of fascinatin' things to see in Frisco. What say you come on along with us; we'll show you the sights. How about it?"

"Thanks just the same. Like I said I'm waiting to meet somebody."

"Well you've been waiting quite a while. Maybe your friend's decided to stand you up, friend."

"I'll just wait a while longer and see."

"Wouldn't take long to see the best part of Frisco. It's all right around here."

Gabe put his hand in his hip pocket and clutched the knuckle-duster, out of sight of the two guys. "Thanks just the same," he said again, and he put an edge on his voice this time while he inspected them more closely. They both looked like the sort who lit sulfur matches on their jaws, but there was a little difference here and there. The one who did most of the talking was slightly higher and wider than the other one. He was also somewhat gamier—a fact to which the breeze attested every time Gabe got to his leeward side. In fact, he smelled like either a whole buffalo herd or a wolf that hadn't been rained on in three months. If he took a bath he'd be about twelve pounds lighter; if they didn't they'd soon be after him to pay real estate taxes on all that dirt.

The dirt was caked in his hair, crusted on his skin, imbedded in his clothes. The closer Gabe looked at him the more awed he became. This was definitely the filthiest guy he'd ever seen, and he'd seen them pretty filthy.

The reason he had time to scrutinize them both was that they had stopped pressing him in order to stand and stare at the vicinity of the front door of Mme. Herz's Clothing Emporium behind him. Their expressions changed, and Gabe turned to see what it was they were looking at.

Nothing. Or anyhow next to nothing. The guy who was emerging from the door and looking furtively over his shoulder was not exactly designed physically to strike terror into the hearts of men. In fact he was about the puniest specimen Gabe had seen since he'd stepped ashore.

"Ittzy Herz," the gamy guy whispered in awe. "Look at that, will you? Right out in bare-ass daylight!"

"Jeez, he must've slipped his leash."

Ittzy Herz's face looked as if it could hold a three-day rain. He was a little sorrowful sparrow with no shoulders and a caved-in chest. He had no visible chin. He was dressed in a little round hat and a cheap black suit that looked as if its seams would come apart any minute. His eyes looked like repositories for the anguish of the ages. Gabe had seen a look like that once in the hollow eyes of a ninety-six-year-old slum priest. Maybe you got to feeling that way and looking that way after you'd seen ninety-six years worth of disappointment and had finally come to the conclusion that there was nothing you could do about it.

The only trouble was, Ittzy Herz wasn't ninety-six years old.

In fact it wasn't clear whether he was even old enough to vote. Maybe it was just his diminutive size, but he looked nineteen.

None of which explained why the two tough guys were regarding him with such undisguised awe.

Ittzy Herz either ignored their stares or didn't even notice them. Probably the latter, Gabe judged; the little guy didn't seem to be aware of anything around him at all.

Ittzy Herz turned away from them and walked sorrowfully up the street. When he had gone out of earshot Gabe said, "Who is that guy anyway?"

"You never heard of Ittzy Herz? He's one of the world-famous sights of San Francisco."

The tough seemed to be draping his arm in friendly fashion around Gabe's shoulders. Gabe shifted away, and the guy moved with him. Gabe kept his hand on the knuckleduster in his pocket. He didn't want a donnybrook with these guys—he wasn't sure he could stand the smell—but he was ready if one came. He said, just to keep the conversation friendly, "What's he world-famous for?"

"Just watch him. You'll see."

Gabe moved out of the encircling grasp and looked up the street. Ittzy Herz was leaving the curb to cross the street. A dilapidated junk cart was coming down the street above him, but Ittzy Herz had plenty of room to get across the street ahead of it. But two things happened. First Ittzy's little round hat fell off, and Ittzy bent down to pick it up. Second a piece of white paper blew across the street under the cart-horse's nose, causing it to shy, rear and bolt.

Suddenly the junk cart was a runaway, and Ittzy was square in its path. Gabe stiffened involuntarily, but behind him he heard the gamy guy's unruffled chuckle.

Ittzy Herz didn't even seem to see the cart thundering down at him. He merely stepped aside to avoid dirtying his boot in a horse pie on the cobblestones. It took him to the left a pace. At the same time the cart horse, for no discernible reason, jerked to Ittzy's right and bolted past him up onto the curb, scattering panic-stricken pedestrians like a fox chasing chickens in a barnyard.

Eventually the cartman brought the runaway under control. A lot of people picked themselves up and dusted themselves off and shook their fists and hollered at the cartman.

· 49 ·

Not Ittzy Herz. He didn't seem to realize what a close call he'd had. He was still walking across the street, without hurry. And as he reached the sidewalk a woman leaned out a second-story window and knocked a flowerpot off the sill with her elbow. Gabe opened his mouth to yell a warning because the flowerpot was on a collision course with Ittzy Herz's head.

But somebody had left a bucket on the sidewalk, so that Ittzy Herz had to walk around it. As he did the flowerpot clanged into the bucket, and he strolled on unscathed. Not merely unscathed; he also seemed totally unaware that anything out of the ordinary had happened.

"You just can't beat that little son of a bitch," the gamy guy said with unconcealed admiration.

"I don't get it," Gabe said as the partner eased in closer and hugged his shoulders.

"Old Ittzy," the gamy guy said, "he's the luckiest son of a bitch ever born. You know one time he fell out of a third-story window up at the Odeon, and there just happened to be a hay wagon going by, and he just happened to land in that nice soft hay?"

"Hell that's nothing," the partner said, "I heard a guy tried to roll Ittzy in Dead Man's Alley, but a boa constrictor grabbed the guy just before he was about to sap Ittzy on the head." •

Gabe said, "A boa constrictor?"

"Yeah, some clown had it in a circus wagon, and it escaped that night. They found it next morning wedged into a hole in the back fence. Seems it couldn't fit through because it had this huge lump in its middle, where it swallowed the guy that'd tried to roll Ittzy."

"Nobody's tried to lay a finger on Ittzy since then," the gamy guy said. He was around on Gabe's other side and getting closer. Gabe's nostrils wrinkled.

The partner said, "I'll tell you, friend, Ittzy's so lucky

his mother keeps him locked up in a room in the back of the store here. She charges people twenty-five cents just to *look* at him through a hole in the door."

"And people pay it," the gamy guy said. "They figure maybe a little luck'll rub off on them too."

Gabe was trying very hard not to breathe at all. "Kind of stuffy right here, wouldn't you say?" And he shook off the partner's arm, took two quick paces out to the edge of the curb, and dragged in a deep breath while he was upwind of them.

The two guys looked at each other. The gamy guy shrugged, the partner nodded. Then the gamy guy pulled a sack out from under his coat. "You know what I got in this sack?"

"It looks empty to me," Gabe said.

"Well just take a closer look."

"GABE!"

They all three looked up, startled. Here came Vangie. She was waving a wallet in front of her as if to shoo away horse-flies. "You two get away from him. Get away! Go on——git!"

The two guys looked at each other. The gamy guy shook his head, the partner shrugged.

Vangie hurried across the street. "Go on. On the run, before I call the police."

"Yeah," the gamy guy said, "that'll be the day." His lip curled. "This dude belong to you, Miss Kemp?"

"Yes. And I'll thank you to keep——"

"All right—all right. We'll do you a little favor this time." The gamy guy stuffed the empty sack back under his coat and made as if to tip his hat but only tugged at the brim a little. He said to Gabe, "All right, friend, we'll take our leave. But a word of advice—you hang around this female, you better count your fingers every time she touches your hand." And the two of them turned and sloped off.

Gabe felt a lot better without those birds crowding him

· *51* ·

the way they had. He said, "What was that all about any-how?"

"Roscoe and his partner? They're crimps."

"Crimps? What's that?"

"They shanghai people. To get crews for the ships."

Gabe paled. "To go on the *ocean*?"

"An awful lot of sailors jump ship when they get to San Francisco," she said. "They all want to head for the gold fields. So the ships need crews, and that means there's good money to be made in crimping."

"Oh, I couldn't take the ocean," Gabe said.

"Good thing I came back when I did." She seemed calmer than necessary, under the circumstances. Handing him the wallet she'd been brandishing, she said, "Here. Now come buy me dinner."

Ittzy Herz was happy. He was out on his own and that was a rare treat. His Mama kept saying all the time, "Ittzy, you got to stay home where it's safe, people always want to take advantage of you. You got to stay home in your room where it's safe." Never had a man had such a protective Mama, and never had a man needed one less.

He didn't mind sitting in the back room while the rubes paid a quarter to look in at him through the peephole. It made him feel important. And it gave him time to read, play solitaire, and think about where he'd go and what he'd do when he was finally free for good. What he minded most was Mama fussing over him all the time. And maybe even worse than that was the times when store business was brisk and peephole business was slack—like it had been tonight. Mama would make him put on an apron and get behind the counter just like everybody else in the family.

Ittzy didn't like that at all. After all he was in show business.

So today when her back was turned he'd scooted out of

his apron and out of the store. And here he was: free. It was the first time he'd run away in quite a while, and it was just as much fun as always. All the people gawking at him, trying to touch him, fawning over him as if he were royalty.

He didn't quite know what all the fuss was about. Everybody seemed to think Ittzy led a charmed life. Well, his father before he'd died had been fond of reading from the Book, and it said right in the Book that a man had threescore years and ten. So Ittzy knew he still had plenty of years to live. The Book said so. What was everybody so surprised about? Ittzy was only thirty-four years old—he still had thirty-six to go.

He stopped into the Golden Rule Saloon for a beer and people crowded one another aside at the bar to get near him. Ittzy saw people he knew and he waved to them the way he'd seen opera stars wave from their open coaches to the applauding crowds they passed.

Over at a table with a skinny Easterner and a whole lot of food was a nice girl named Evangeline Kemp whom Ittzy knew slightly. He waved to her and she waved back with a pretty smile, and Ittzy felt good. He thought he might write a poem about a pretty girl's smile. It sounded like a good original idea, and he began to work out the wording in his head. He'd written thousands of poems. Someday someone would recognize his genius and publish one of them.

A big fellow with an enormous moustache came rolling into the saloon and slugged his way to the bar near Ittzy, although Ittzy had the feeling the man hadn't seen or recognized him. The man slammed a hammerlike fist down on the bar and roared, "Anybody around here sell anything that'd approximate a drink?"

Ittzy sipped his beer and basked in all the admiring attention he was getting. But he glanced from time to time at the guy with the huge moustache, who was just about the only person in the room who didn't seem to have noticed Ittzy's presence. It bothered Ittzy to have somebody who didn't know who he was. Especially since he was sure he'd seen that face before.

The big fellow's drink was delivered by a sweating barkeep and the guy took a healthy swallow, almost gagging on it. He said hoarsely, "Christ, they seem to be puttin' bigger snakes in these here bottles this season." His eyes were watering and he shoved his face into the crook of his elbow to wipe his eyes on his sleeve. When he dropped his arm his eyes lit on Ittzy for the first time. He froze.

Ittzy began to smile, enjoying his little triumph, even if it was belated. At least the guy recognized him now.

The guy with the moustache stared at him without blinking—without even seeming to breathe. Then his face slowly changed. It got dark, suffused with blood. The big jaw under the moustache crept forward to lie in a grim belligerent line. The guy's hand dropped off the bar and he suddenly bent over, lifting one foot.

Ittzy couldn't figure out what the man was doing. But then he saw he was working the boot off his foot.

Finally the boot came off and the big fellow turned and hobbled toward Ittzy on one booted foot and one dirty-socked foot.

Ittzy frowned.

The guy with the moustache came right up to him, elbowing everybody else out of his way, and shouted right in Ittzy's face, "You're the fellow sold me this boot!"

Ittzy just looked at him. He couldn't figure out what the fellow was getting at.

The big man waved the boot in Ittzy's face, and the sole flapped open and shut as though it were the boot talking instead of the man. "This is what you sold me!" the big fellow said (or the boot said). "What you aim to do about it?"

"Me?" Ittzy didn't think of it as his problem; it wasn't his boot, and it wasn't his store. "Nothing," he said, turning back to his beer.

The big fellow grabbed his elbow. "I say you sold me this boot!" he yelled.

"Did I?"

"You're damn right you did! *Two hours ago!*"

Ittzy smiled in friendly fashion. "Maybe you better talk to my Mama," he said. "It's her store."

"I'm talking to you!" the big fellow yelled, flapping the boot some more like a ventriloquist. "*You're* the one sold me this boot!"

"I'm just trying to drink my beer here," Ittzy said, still working at being friendly.

"You got to make good on this!"

"My Mama doesn't put any guarantee on her goods."

"*Two hours!*"

Ittzy shook his head and went back to his beer. All he wanted was a little peace and quiet in which to enjoy this rare moment of freedom before his Mama came looking for him, as inevitably she would.

But the big fellow yanked him around yet again by the elbow and this time instead of the boot he had a gun in his hand. He wave dthe big old mean-looking .45-caliber revolver in Ittzy's face. "Well, gee whiz," Ittzy said, in mild complaint.

The big fellow was breathing pretty hard, but he did try to keep his voice at a reasonable level. "I want to know what you're going to do about that boot," he said.

"Well," Ittzy said helplessly, "just nothing, I guess."

"You're asking for it."

"I'd admire to finish this beer."

The big fellow's big thumb curled over the hammer of the

.45 and drew it back to full cock. "You're gonna get it!" he yelled, no longer trying to control his voice.

Ittzy shrugged, and turned away to address himself once more to his beer. Everybody in the saloon was bolt still and silent. He wished the big fellow would go somewhere else. There was nothing Ittzy could do to help him out, which he'd already explained, so why didn't he just take his boot and his gun and hop off to pester somebody else for a while?

But he didn't. Instead, he yelled at the top of his voice, "All *right!*" and yanked Ittzy around by his elbow for about the twentieth time. Then he fired that big .45 revolver point blank at Ittzy from two feet away.

It was a terrible noise, up so close like that. Ittzy blinked, and the gent at the bar next to him said, "Uhh," and folded slowly forward, fading down onto the floor.

Everybody looked at the gent on the floor. The fellow with the gun in his hand cocked his head to one side, as though listening to something he didn't understand, and said, "George? Not you, George, *him*. George?"

There was a lot of ruckus in the bar. Ittzy frowned and picked up his beer to finish it, since he doubted he'd have much more time to sit here in quiet and contentment. That poor sport with the talking boot sure could louse up a man's afternoon off.

The bar had gotten completely silent just before the shooting, but just after it everybody had started talking at once. Now all of a sudden everything was quiet again. Ittzy turned around to see what had happened, and another actor had entered the scene. It was a very tall skinny cop with bright red hair sticking out from under his bobby helmet; he had bustled into the Golden Rule and stopped just inside to appraise the situation.

Ittzy was at the bar and the big fellow with the moustache was down on one knee saying, "George? George?" The smoking gun in his right fist was forgotten. Everybody else had crowded back away, leaving a little open space around them.

The cop pushed his way through to the open circle. He was talking, wanting to know what was going on, who fired that shot, what happened.

A dozen people started explaining things, all at the same time. And from the edges of the circle, other customers began to drift Ittzyward. In a city full of transients possessed by gold fever, a guaranteed good-luck charm could draw a bigger crowd than a shooting.

They started to touch him. A hand would reach out of the crowd and pluck at his sleeve. Somebody's finger touched his cheek. Someone whispered, "You be my good luck charm too, huh Ittzy? Huh?"

Ittzy concentrated, as best he could, on his beer.

Somebody said, "Well at least George ain't dead. I guess he'll pull through. Get him right over to the nearest doctor, will you?" It sounded like the cop talking, but the crowd had jammed in around Ittzy and he couldn't see. Then the cop was saying, presumably to the big fellow, "You, there, you're under arrest for assault and disturbing the peace and attempted murder."

"ITTZY!"

Oh no. He closed his eyes in misery. It was Mama's voice, you couldn't mistake that claxon.

The two of them approached him at the same time from different directions, the tall red-haired cop and Mama. They reached him simultaneously, and the cop opened his mouth to speak. But Mama quick grabbed Itzzy's ear and pulled him off his stool. "Now," she yelled, "you come right home with me!"

The cop said, "Hey. Wait a minute. I want to question this here witness."

Mama turned and leveled her ferocious stare on the cop. "You want to see my boy Ittzy up close, Officer McCorkle, you come around my shop and pay twenty-five cents, the fourth part of a dollar, just like everbody else."

"Oh, Mama," Ittzy said.

Mama took a firmer grip on his ear and headed for the door.

7

Gabe watched Ittzy's mother lead Ittzy toward the door. "Maybe I ought to go touch him too."

Vangie said, "Why?"

"If a fellow wants to be in New York and finds himself stuck in San Francisco, what kind of luck would you call that?"

"Better than the fellow deserved," she said. "You finished eating?"

Gabe looked at all his empty plates. Four of them. "I believe I am."

The red-haired cop, McCorkle, was dragging the kicking and howling moustachioed guy out. Ittzy and his mother were gone. The crowd was separating into smaller excited knots of people, everybody talking at once. Vangie said, "I hope there's enough in that wallet to pay the bill for all this."

It was something he hadn't thought to investigate. He fumbled the wallet open anxiously.

It was all right. There were two five-dollar greenjackets in the wallet. He paid the supper tab and still had five dollars and fifty-five cents, of which minus–$4.45 belonged to *him*.

This wouldn't do. He was going to have to get himself in motion; he couldn't spend the rest of his life living off this girl's ingenuity. "Let's get out of here."

"Where to?"

He was trying to think but it was no good. The heaps of food with which he'd filled himself had replenished most of what he'd lost on the river, but it didn't make him any more alert and wide-eyed. Seasickness took a lot out of you.

"I need sleep before I can start making plans. Let's check out those hotel rooms of yours."

"Right," Vangie said. Leaving the table, they threaded a path through the crowd and emerged onto the street.

It was dark. A cold breeze swept past them, stirring tendrils of fog. Gaslights were encircled by vague misty halos and the people who went by were sinister moving shadows. Gabe shivered. "Which way?"

"We'll try up here first."

The climb made New York's Washington Heights seem like a molehill by comparison. What idiot had decided to put a would-be city on the side of a cliff? Out here in the West they just didn't know how to do *anything* right.

"Where are you from anyway?"

"You mean where was I born?" Vangie asked. "On Mission Street in a second-story flat across the street from the church."

"Mission Street where?"

She looked at him as they crossed an intersection. "What do you mean where? Right down there." She pointed down the hill behind them.

"You mean you were *born* in San Francisco?"

"Of course."

He did some rapid arithmetic. Well, it was possible after all. The gold had been discovered in 1848; they must have started building this excuse for a city right after that. That was twenty-six years ago.

"It isn't there any more," she said.

He was beginning to puff from the climb. "What isn't?"

"The place where I was born. It burned down in the fire of fifty-four."

Which narrowed things down to a six-year span. So she wasn't younger than twenty, and she wasn't older than twenty-six. Gabe began to feel fiendishly clever.

But she shattered this feeling. "I'm twenty-four, if that's what you're trying to figure out."

"Did I ask?" he demanded. "Did I?"

"How old are you?"

"What difference does that make?"

"Well, I just asked. You don't have to throw a fit." She stopped so abruptly that he banged into her. He looked up at a bulky five-story building. Vangie said, "Let's try this one."

Gabe headed for the porticoed door, but Vangie dragged him back by the sleeve. "Not that way. Come on."

Around the side of the building. Past dark windows and a rubbish pile. Finally she turned and pulled open a door that Gabe wouldn't have seen in the dark alley.

A dimly lit corridor. Kitchen smells, the sound of rattling utensils in a dishpan. Vangie led him stealthily past the kitchen door and up a rickety flight of backstairs, keeping her weight on the inner edge of the treads and motioning to Gabe to do the same.

She preceded him up the stairs and stopped at a door on the landing. "I'll check first," she whispered. "They may have rented it to somebody else."

He waited, holding the stairway door ajar and watching her tiptoe down the carpeted hall to a door. She slipped the key into the lock. He heard the faint click of the latch and then Vangie disappeared inside.

Almost instantly she flew out into the corridor, followed

by an irate shriek. She rushed back down the corridor and fled past him. Gabe pulled the stairway door shut.

He didn't catch up until they had reached the alley. Vangie gave him an embittered look. "You wouldn't believe what that woman was wearing to bed. All right, the next one's just a block over. Come on."

Gabe stood at the head of the backstairs, very winded and very tired. He hoped desperately that this one would be all right because it was at the top of a six-story hotel and he just didn't have the strength to go on climbing hills and stairs for the rest of the night.

But there was a scream and his face fell.

Then he recognized the voice. It was Vangie screaming this time.

Gabe rushed across the corridor and collided with Vangie as she came pell-mell out of the room, skirts flying and followed by a long-armed miner in long johns.

The miner was leering at the fleeing girl and didn't seem to see Gabe. There was only a split second while the miner roared past him, but Gabe used it to whip the knuckle-duster out of his pocket and apply it to the rear of the miner's head.

He fell down and began to curl up like a strip of frying bacon.

Gabe took Vangie's arm and hustled her down the stairs. On the street she stopped to get her breath; she tipped her head back to look at him. "My goodness. You're faster than the telegraph."

"Well, you know back East in New York, where——"

"Where men are men. Yes, I know."

"Yeah. Well. Your luck seems to be about as good as mine. Maybe we ought to go pay the twenty-five cents to see Ittzy."

"Well there's still one hotel left. This way."

He followed her to the curb and they set foot in the street, about to cross it. But a sudden clamor of bells clanged nearby.

The street instantly cleared of people. Vangie dashed for the nearest doorway while Gabe, still in the middle of the street, looked around, baffled. The bells were getting louder.

"Gabe!" Vangie yelled, from the protection of the doorway. "Run for it!"

He was about to, even though he still didn't know why, when another voice from another direction called in accents of surprise and joy, "Why, Gabe! How *are* you? It's been *years!*"

Vangie shouted, "Gabe—come on!"

He looked back and forth in confusion. The bells jangled and clanged. Vangie stood in her doorway with one hand extended, beseeching him. From the other way—across the street—a willowy young man, rather overdressed, came strolling forward out of the fog with smile and hand both outstretched.

"Well, I'll be damned," Gabe said. "Francis Calhoun."

Francis Calhoun approached, smiling, saying something else that was lost in the racket of the bells. From the other side, Vangie came rushing back out to yank Gabe to safety. And all at once something came around the corner, big, loud and fast. It tore hell for leather in their direction.

A fire engine. The biggest, fastest, reddest horse-drawn fire engine in the entire world—bell clanging, white horses raging, wheels clattering, the whole mess hurtling their way like a falling roof. Gabe stood there in the middle of the street, Francis Calhoun on one side of him and Vangie on the other, and like an avalanche at Grand Canyon the fire engine roared on by.

The wind of its passage all but knocked Gabe to the ground. He yelled something, but even he himself couldn't hear what it was. Then the thing was past and careening on down the hill, gathering its noise around itself like coattails.

Gabe blinked. He looked around in the dust cloud the

thing had left in its wake, and damn if Vangie wasn't still there. Damn if Francis Calhoun wasn't still there. Gabe looked down at himself; damn if *he* wasn't still there.

"Oh, my goodness," Vangie said faintly.

Francis, dusty but unruffled, continued to wear his welcoming smile as he said, "How are you, old cock?"

Gabe looked down the street. A few blocks below, the fire engine roared around a corner, swaying far over, not quite capsizing, righting itself, and swooping on out of sight and gradually out of hearing. Past that corner, straight on down all the way to the waterfront, the street was as empty as Tenth Avenue after a shot has been fired. "Now, what——" he said, then swallowed and tried again. "Just what in hell was that?"

"Fire engine," Francis said, wrinkling his nose in distaste. "That garish color," he said.

Gabe turned to Vangie for a fuller explanation. "What was it?"

A pale Vangie clutched her throat. "The closest I've ever been to being posthumous," she said.

Gabe said, "We've got fire engines back in New York, too, but not like *that*."

Vangie said, "Gabe, this city's burned down twice so far. You can say what you want about San Francisco, but the people here aren't stupid. We do get the point after a while, so now we've got ourselves the finest, fastest, most modern fire engines in any city in the whole world."

"Clang, clang," Francis said disapprovingly. "You wouldn't believe how they carry on."

Vangie peered curiously past Gabe at Francis. "I don't think I——"

"Nor have I," Francis said. "Do introduce us, Gabe."

"Yeah," Gabe said reluctantly. "Uh, Vangie Kemp, this here is Francis Calhoun. I, uh, used to know him back in New York."

"One of my *dearest* friends," Francis said. "Was that Angie or Vangie, dear?"

"E–van–ge–line," Vangie said, smiling with her teeth.

Gabe looked all around, making a point of not meeting Francis' eye. "Well," he said, "it looks safe now. I guess we can all move on, huh?"

Francis was saying, "Dear Gabe and I grew up together. Didn't we, Gabe?"

"Yeah, that's right," Gabe said. He was ready to depart from there, call the conversation quits, and have nothing more to do with Francis Calhoun forever. It was true they'd grown up in the same neighborhood, but they hadn't exactly been together. Having little interest in beating up the weak and defenseless just for the fun of it—as opposed to doing so for profit—Gabe had been one of the very few children in the neighborhood who hadn't gone out of his way to make Francis Calhoun's youth memorable. If Francis now looked back on that inactivity and remembered it as a deep and abiding friendship that was his own business, but Gabe wanted no part of it.

But Vangie was saying, through that rather odd, toothy set smile, "Well, any friend of Gabe's is a friend of mine."

"My feeling exactly," Francis said. His own smile didn't seem to have any teeth in it at all; his lips curved limply, like a couple of anchovies on a plate.

"I guess that must be an Eastern suit," Vangie said, aiming her smile at his loud clawhammer coat.

"I'm glad you like it," Francis said, preening a bit. His clothes were flamboyantly cheap and somewhat the worse for wear. The worn coat was shiny here and there, but the colors were nearly blinding at this close range. Over it he wore a short cape with a bright pink lining. His dark hair was all wet down, and he gave the general appearance of a lunatic undertaker or an apprentice carnival barker. Drawing a lace-fringed handkerchief now from the cuff of his coat and dusting himself off, he said, "One does pick up so much dirt in the street, doesn't one? Did you say you were a local girl?"

She smiled sweetly. "I didn't say. Do you spell Francis with an i or an e?"

"Well, that does depend."

For a reason he didn't entirely understand, these two were making Gabe very nervous. Before either of them could say anything more, he stepped between them, took Vangie's arm, and said, "Nice seeing you again, Francis. We'll have to have a drink sometime and talk over the old days."

"An excellent suggestion," Francis said, taking Gabe's other arm. "And no time like the present. Shall we go somewhere for an apéritif?"

Francis regarded the waiter with some mistrust. "Have you ever heard," he inquired, "of a Pink Lady?"

"You probably want one of them hotel dives down by the waterfront," the waiter said.

Francis sighed. Even here in the plush saloon of one of the big hilltop hotels, surrounded by city fathers in black coats and railroad men smoking cigars, one had to deal with the plebeian mind. "A Pink Lady," he explained loftily, "is a form of beverage. Ask your bartender, perhaps he has experience of it."

"A Pink," the waiter said, "Lady." He had the beetle-browed look of a man who's put up with a lot in his life and maybe isn't going to put up with much more. He eyed the trio at the table as though thinking of falling on them. Heavily he said, "Pink Ladies for everybody?"

"Sounds as though I might like it," the girl Evangeline said. She was sitting there with her elbow on the table and her forearm straight up and pinkie crooked as though she were holding a teacup at the vicar's. Every time Francis caught her eye she gave him the same set smile.

The waiter looked at Gabe flatly. "You, too?"

"Whisky," Gabe growled. "In a glass."

It would take more than that to improve the waiter's disposition. Wordlessly he turned and went away.

Francis leaned back and looked around the large genteel room, its quiet muffled by money and mohair. He had brought dear old Gabe and Gabe's little urchin friend here because he felt the frank need for a little beauty around himself.

Times had been difficult lately; in fact, they'd been terrible. Francis had come out here from New York three years ago to make a fresh start with new friends in a setting more amicably attuned to his nature than New York City's rough-and-tumble. Of course he'd had his ups and downs since then, of which the ups had never been extraordinarily high, but the downs had tended to be bone-crushing. And the current depression looked as though it might turn out to be the worst of them all.

Dimly he heard the girl talking to Gabe, extolling the wonders of San Francisco: two thousand saloons and blind pigs, she was saying, or one for every seventy-six inhabitants. There were three thousand Chinese girls in the city, she said, who had been imported as bordello slaves by the vice lords of the Chinese Tongs.

She went on in that vein. Francis hardly understood her point; it seemed in execrable taste, but what could one expect after all? The Lord knew that Francis had tried to instill an appreciation of the finer things in this wilderness encampment, but it was hard going—ever so hard.

He leaned forward again, waited for a pause in the girl's recital of the less appetizing local statistics, and then said, "Well, Gabe old cock, it really is wonderful to see you again."

"Yeah."

"You've come out West to make your fortune, I bet."

"You bet."

"Well, I've never regretted coming out, I can tell you that." Francis smiled in easy self-deprecation and said, "Not that I've become one of your local millionaires, don't get me wrong."

"I wouldn't do that," Gabe said.

"But the city itself," Francis said, "is *très jolie*. And the people—well, there are rough edges to them, of course, but deep down they're really quite a tolerant lot. Far more so than back East."

"Yeah."

"I *have* been making my living," he said, emphasizing the past tense, "as a designer. Fashion, you know."

The girl's smile thawed a little. "Ladies' fashions?"

"In a way," Francis told her. "Designs for the theater, you know."

She looked more and more interested. "The theater?"

"The cancan shows, in fact," Francis said. He said it proudly, though he knew there were those who misunderstood the visual element in the cancan shows, and thought of them as nothing but unredeemed sex. He himself knew better and was prepared to defend the shows at the drop of a sneer.

But the girl didn't sneer. Leaning closer she said, "That must be real interesting," and Francis realized that, like most women, this girl Evangeline was stagestruck.

"Oh, it is," Francis said. "Or it has been, at any rate. Unfortunately the Philistines just closed us again. They do that every so often." To Gabe he said, "You may have seen the posters Xed out all over town."

"Yeah, I think I did." Gabe was spending most of his time looking around the room, waiting for his drink; it was the girl who was doing the listening.

Nevertheless, it was to Gabe that Francis preferred to address himself. "This city," he said, "is full of gambling, harlots, swindlers, and an array of vice you wouldn't *believe,*

Gabe. I mean, it's absolutely wide *open*. Not that I object personally; I mean, live and let live is my *motto*. But every once in a while the city fathers go on a puritan spree, announcing they're going to clean up the whole city and turn us into some sort of *Boston* or something—and what do they wind up doing? They close the cancan shows!"

"Yeah," Gabe said, looking around the room.

"Even out on the frontier," Francis said sadly, "men are full of hypocrisy."

"Yeah, probably."

At that point the waiter finally came back with the drinks and thudded them onto the table, one by one. Then he stood there waiting.

Francis looked at Gabe and saw Gabe looking back at him. He looked at the girl, and she too was looking at him. Even the waiter was looking at him.

"Oh, dear," Francis said.

"I thought so," the waiter said.

Francis felt terribly embarrassed. "Gabe, I thought . . . Well, I did tell you we'd been closed down, I thought you understood, uh——"

Gabe said, without expression, "You don't have any money."

"I've been in dreadful financial shape these past few weeks."

"Right," the waiter said. He started putting the drinks back on the tray.

"Hold it, you," Gabe said. He produced a wallet from his overstuffed pockets, turned it around a bit in his hands as though unfamiliar with how to get into it, and then slid a bill at the waiter. Francis caught a flash of a five-dollar green-jacket.

After the waiter had made change and gone heavily away, Francis said, "The worst of it is, I wouldn't be in this awkward condition if it weren't for some utter scoundrels who lied to me."

"Is that so," Gabe said.

"But it did seem such a marvelous opportunity at the time," Francis insisted. "I couldn't pass it up, you know. I mean, you could actually see the glinting veins of it on the surface of the shaft wall."

The girl gave him a look. "You bought a gold mine."

Francis nodded. "Like a fool I trusted them. Well, one in particular. I couldn't *believe* that after—well, I just didn't think he'd treat me that way."

"They'd salted it?"

"Not really. They'd played the mine out, that's all. A few traces of gold left, but they'd emptied out all the worthwhile ore. It's nothing but a gutted hole in the hillside now. And like a fool I sank *all* my savings in it, only to find it's as empty as a drummer's promises."

Gabe lifted his glass and Francis caught a hard gleam in his eye. "Anyhow," Gabe said, "here's to gold. Lots of gold."

"Oh my, yes," Francis agreed.

The girl gave Gabe a bit of a mulish look, he noticed, but she drank.

Gabe leaned closer to Francis. "Listen, do you know many guys around this burg?"

"Why old cock, I know everybody, just *every*body."

"Well, I'm looking into something big, and I might need some good people to help out."

Francis smiled. "Just like the old days."

"Um," said Gabe.

The girl gave Gabe a suspicious look and said, "Is it still that same idea?"

"Sure," he said. "I didn't use it up yet."

"Well, I wish you would," she said. "You're just going to go along bullheaded and not listen to anybody else that knows more about things around here than you do. The first thing you know you're going to get yourself in a lot of trouble."

Gabe tucked his head down in like a man who's made a

conscious decision to be stubborn and said, "I know what I'm doing."

Alarmed on Gabe's behalf, Francis turned to the girl and said, "Is it really dangerous?"

Now she too was looking stubborn. "Dangerous," she echoed. "It's goddam *stupid*, is what it is."

"We'll see about that," Gabe said.

Francis touched the girl's wrist. "My dear," he said, "you can't stop a man if he's determined to go ahead and do something. Believe me I've tried, and it just can't be done."

"Don't I know it," she said. "You can talk yourself blue in the face."

"Exactly," Francis said, in long-suffering sympathy.

Their eyes met, with identical rueful expressions. They lifted their Pink Ladies and smiled at one another in perfect warmth and understanding. She was, he realized, much better than he had at first thought.

Across the room a cattleman in a huge hat turned his head and spat something into a bell-mounted brass-bellied spittoon. The clang echoed throughout the ornate room. Francis winced.

Gabe said, "Francis, you want to keep in touch with me."

"Where are you staying?"

Gabe and the girl looked at each other. Francis couldn't quite fathom the expression that passed between them. Finally Gabe said, "Well we'll be around, one place and another. Where can I reach you?"

"I have a room on Kearny Street. Twenty-eight and a half. I have the entire top floor."

The girl said, "I imagine it's fixed up grand."

"Well, a few touches perhaps."

Gabe was pouring himself another whisky, distracted evidently by private thoughts. Francis sought to revive the conversation; gold had been mentioned and he wanted to dwell on that, but there was something else to be covered. "You certainly are a long way from home, old cock," he said.

"Yeah. So are you."

"To be sure. The difference being, I can go back."

He let it drop in a very casual tone, watching closely as Gabe picked it up and examined it.

Finally Gabe said, "I don't believe it."

The girl looked at him. "You don't believe what?"

Gabe ignored her. He put his glass of whisky down and faced Francis with an I-should-have-known nod. "So Twill got in touch with you."

"I've never been so surprised as when I got his telegram," Francis said. "I mean, he's hardly my type, old Patrick Twill." He screwed up his face and shivered. "Fat ugly old——"

"Twill," Gabe said, pronouncing the word as if it were chipped out of hard steel.

Francis turned both palms up on the table. "I thought I should be open and aboveboard about it, Gabe old cock. I'm not concealing anything from you."

"What about it then?"

"He wired me. Just said he wanted to know if I was still in San Francisco, because there would be a bit of money in it if I replied to his wire. So I did, seeing no harm in it. Behold, there came a second telegram from Twill. He wired me twenty-five dollars, of which I was sorely in need at that particular juncture. He said I would receive an additional fifty dollars if I would watch for your arrival and wire him as soon as you appeared."

"And?"

"And what?"

"That's not all of it, Francis."

"Well, there was only one further instruction. If you left San Francisco with any evident intention of returning East,

I was to wire him again and advise him of your approach. For this of course I would receive a further reward."

"And did you wire him when I arrived?"

"Certainly. I watched the arrivals today and saw you come ashore. I went to the telegraph office immediately and sent the wire. Unfortunately by the time I returned to the docks you had disappeared, and I've been looking for you ever since."

"To tell me about Twill?"

"Well, not entirely. I mean you *are* one of my very dearest friends, old cock."

"Yeah."

"Have I done something wrong?"

"I guess not," Gabe said. "But one of these days I'm going back East, Francis, and I'm going to jerk that Persian carpet right out from under Fat Pat Twill. When I do I don't want any telegraph messages going out to warn him I'm coming back. You got that clear?"

"Well, I——"

"You'll be rich enough by the time I leave," Gabe said, "that you won't need any crumbs from Twill. I promise you that."

"Rich? Me?"

"We're all gonna be rich. You just stick by me and get ready to jump when I say frog."

The girl, as if to head off Gabe from a topic she disliked, said quickly, "This Twill—who's he?"

"Just a guy," Gabe growled.

Francis smiled. "He's better known as Boss Twill, king of the underworld on the West Side of New York."

She turned to lay her hand across Gabe's arm on the table. "So that's why you left New York. You were in danger from this big shot. You're not really going *back* there?"

"When I'm ready," Gabe said. He seemed to be trying to

lift his glass, but the girl was holding his arm down. He turned a glare on her. "Look, nothing you can say or do is going to change my mind, so forget it." He swiveled the glare toward Francis and Francis sat a little lower in the chair. "And you. Some associate."

"Associate?"

"Never mind," Gabe said. "Look, are you in or out?"

"In what?"

"With me. To get rich. Or are you satisfied being Twill's errand-boy associate for twenty-five bucks a telegram?"

Francis really didn't have to consider it very hard. He was getting very sick and tired of living on the economic fringes. Gabe had talked about gold; Twill hadn't mentioned anything of the kind.

He said, "Well of *course* I'm in, old cock, if my talents can be employed profitably."

"Okay. I'll be in touch." And abruptly Gabe got to his feet, lifted the girl out of her chair, and steered her toward the door.

9

As they went out, Vangie looked back from the door at the thin fey dude smiling at them from the table, waving his Pink Lady with cool insouciance. He had been a surprise to her, in a lot of different ways.

On the street she said to Gabe, "I like your friend."

"Um," he said.

"I didn't think I would at first. But he's really kind of nice."

"Um," Gabe said. He stood there squinting down the street as though he wasn't really a part of this conversation.

Vangie studied him, thinking he had to be a more complex character than she had at first supposed. Not a simple Eastern roughneck after all, if he had artistic friends like Francis Calhoun. "I'm surprised you and he are such good friends," she said.

"Yeah," Gabe said. "It kind of surprised me, too."

"I bet his flat is lovely."

"Yeah. Probably. Listen, what about that hotel room?"

"We've got one place left to try," she said. "If that's no good we can go back down and check the keybox again."

"That's fine," he said. He didn't sound as if he meant it.

"What's the matter?"

"The thought of going all the way down to the docks and then all the way back up these hills again."

"You'll get used to it."

"Not me," he said. "I don't intend to stay here long enough to have to."

It troubled her the way he kept talking like that. She didn't quite know why but she didn't want to lose him. She wondered if, when the time came, he'd ask her to go back to New York with him. And if he did, she wondered if she would. She felt about New York roughly the same way she felt about San Francisco.

She took him around the corner into Powell Street and waited for the cable car; when it came clanging by they got on it and rode up toward Nob Hill. She explained the cable car to Gabe; he didn't seem overcome by enthusiasm—he kept looking back from the open platform down the steep hill and making remarks about what would happen if the cable car slipped off its rails and cable.

It was one of the small exclusive Nob Hill hotels she was heading for, and she didn't hold out much hope. But she took Gabe there anyway, left him again at the stairs, and walked down the corridor boldly enough. At first this kind of thing had terrified her, but she'd learned it was easy enough to avoid trouble by acting sweet and innocent. She had the key to the wrong room—they must have made a mistake at the desk. That was all there was to it.

Still, there was always that second's hesitation just before inserting the key in the lock.

But this time she forced herself to act without a pause. She was aware of Gabe's eyes on her from the other end of the corridor, and her feelings for him seemed to have deepened in a way that amazed her.

She opened the door, stepped quickly inside, and found the

room empty. She checked the closet and under the bed, and found no luggage; so they hadn't rented it again. She went back to the door and signaled to Gabe to join her.

He came hurrying on tiptoe and whispered when he got to her, "Is it okay?"

"It's fine," she said, in a normal voice. "Come on in."

He came in and looked around, and it seemed to her she could detect disapproval in his expression. It was true it wasn't a very good room, definitely one of the cheaper accommodations in this hotel—very small, with a pockmarked brass bed that looked more than ordinarily lumpy, and a narrow window that looked out on nothing but another wall half a dozen feet away. The porcelain pitcher and bowl were both cracked, the dresser drawers were missing half their handles, and there wasn't so much as a throw rug on the wide plank floor.

"It isn't much of a room," she said, suddenly awkward and sheepish with this fellow she'd met only today, even though this was hardly the first time she'd been alone in a hotel room with a man.

"It's all right," he said, shrugging and moving to look out the window.

"I'm sorry it doesn't have a view," she said. "I'll try to do better tomorrow."

He nodded, turning away from the window. "Yeah, I'd like that," he said. "I'd like a view."

"You would?"

"Yeah. A view of the Mint."

Feeling both irritated and disappointed, she said, "Aren't you ever going to give that up?"

"Not for a second," he said. He shucked out of his coat and hung it neatly on the back of the room's only chair. "In fact," he said, "you can take me up there and show me the place. Do they have tours for the public, anything like that?"

"Gabe, I wish you'd——"

"Do they?"

She sighed and nodded. "Yes."

"Good."

"Maybe it's just as well," she said. "You'll see for yourself it's impossible to break in there."

He grinned as though he didn't believe it. "Then I'll give up, won't I?"

"I don't know. Will you?"

He came over, still grinning, and touched the line of her jaw with two fingertips. His finger pads were smooth and soft, not like the horny calluses of most men out here; though the feeling couldn't be described as feminine either. Touching her that way, still grinning, he said, "You seem to be fretting over me."

She felt foolish and more than a little weak. "Damn it anyway, Gabe," she said, and tried to turn her face away from his touch.

"Vangie?" His fingers slid along the line of her jaw, under her ear, and pushed into her hair, insistent and yet gentle. His fingers and palm cupped the back of her head, enmeshed in her hair, and drew her slowly but unresistingly forward until their lips touched.

It was a long kiss but not a violent one. She wanted to reach up and put her arms around him, but she held back, afraid of being too easy, boring him, or scaring him away. When at last they separated, she whispered, "It wouldn't be the first saddle I've known, Gabe."

His voice more hoarse than usual, he said, "Did I ask you?"

"No. But I wanted you to know."

"Neither one of us wants to waste time on a greenhorn," he said, drawing her close again. This time her arms reached up and wrapped around him.

10

The Mint hulked on its hilltop
in the light of the evening sun.
At the window of their new hotel room Gabe stood sizing it
up like a trainer of circus animals peering through the bars
at a tiger he isn't sure he can handle.

Vangie was out somewhere acquiring capital. The sun was
about to go down, which seemed the best time of day for her
enterprising ventures—just after suppertime when people
were a bit sleepy, slow-moving, and not too sensitive around
the pockets.

He had resigned himself to sponging off her. It would only
be for a few days more. He needed the time to set things up
and check things out. Without Vangie he'd have had to get
a job or start rolling drunks, and he didn't want to waste the
time.

He'd been busy enough the past several days. He'd walked
up and down the hills, wandered the city, studied and thought
and observed and pondered. He'd spent a lot of time around
the neighborhood of the Mint, studying it from all sides and
making inquiries. He picked up bits and pieces of vital infor-
mation like the number of privies, the fact that it had been
built in 1854, and the rumor that one of the guards had a

girl friend on Pacific Street as well as a wife in Chinatown. He'd been talking a tough line, particularly where Vangie was concerned, but privately he wasn't sure he could crack it. It was a hell of a forbidding building, that Mint.

Still, the thought of home kept him going. Home, Twill, and Vangie, too—he could hardly back down now; he'd look like a fool in her eyes.

He pulled out his snap-lid watch—Twill's gift—and say it was almost time to go down and meet Vangie at their daily meeting place at Front and Jackson. He began to poke around the hotel room to make sure they hadn't left any possessions behind. Not that there was much to leave. He'd bought a new set of clothes, including a heavy pea jacket to ward off the impressively cold fog that rolled in even more frequently than Vangie had allowed it did. He had also accumulated a spare set of underwear and a few pairs of socks, but they were all wadded into the pockets of the big pea jacket along with his knuckle-duster and the rest of the oddments he'd carried faithfully ever since he'd left civilization. With one last look out the window at the Mint, he left the room to meet up with Vangie.

She was waiting for him at the corner, looking as pert, feisty and cheerful as ever. "Look what I found," she said, drawing him back into the alley mouth to show him her treasure.

It was a silver-plated whisky flask. "Not bad," he said, looking at it as she held it up for him.

"I thought you'd like it. It's a present," she said. She twisted the top to open it, and fired a shot that plugged a hole into the wall next to Gabe's head.

A little later, in another hotel room, when she was a bit calmer, she said, "I just don't know why people walk around with things like that in their pockets. It ought to be against the law. It's making me very nervous."

Gabe, who had taken charge of the flask, was sitting on the bed examining it. "Well, sometimes," he said, distracted by the intricacy of the thing, "it's handy to carry a gun that doesn't look like a gun."

"Well it isn't handy for *me*," she said with a melodramatic shudder. "What *else* is going to blow up in my fingers?"

Gabe nodded over the flask. It hald five .25-caliber rounds loaded through the bottom and fired through the top, when the lid was turned counterclockwise. Very ingenious.

"Gabe?"

"Huh? Oh." He put the flask down on the bed and got to his feet. "Well, let's see. You can find guns built into snuff-boxes, into pipes, or most anything that can be made of metal and small enough to carry in your pocket."

"What is civilization coming to?"

He grinned at her. "Maybe you better just take wallets from now on."

"Someday," she said bitterly, "a wallet will turn out to be a revolver in disguise."

"Well," he said, "you could always change your ways."

"What?"

"Turn over a new leaf," he explained. "Mend the error of your ways."

She said, "You mean go *straight*?"

"Sure."

She made a face, to show she was not amused. "If you can't be serious," she said, "there's no point talking about it."

"Stick to wallets," he told her. "You'll be okay." He gestured toward the flask, lying so innocently on the bed. "Mind if I keep that?"

"Well, *I* don't want it, believe me."

"Thanks," he said.

11

Promptly at the start of visiting hours Vangie and Gabe took a guided tour of the Mint.

She knew it was the only way to persuade him of the impossibility of his idea. Nobody had ever robbed the United States Mint. Nobody in his right mind would dare.

It was a fortress, the Mint, surrounded by a high wall. A guide assembled the visitors at the front gates, which were high wrought-iron affairs you couldn't break down with a five-ton battering ram.

The view from the courtyard inside the high wall was like what the inside view of a prison must be. Stone and masonry thirty feet high surrounded the whole thing. The pair of armed guards at the gate looked as if they'd rather stomp you than eat.

"This branch of the United States Mint opened for business in April of Eighteen and Fifty-four," the guide announced in a pompous voice that made his double chins wobble. "The Gov'ment established the Mint here for the purpose of minting gold coinage, because this is where the gold is, haw haw. Now the coins we stamp here are almost exclusively eagles and double eagles, which as you folks know is ten and twenny dollar coins. Now and then we stamp an issue of five-dollar half eagles, but it don't happen very often here. So if you find a half eagle with our stamp on it maybe you want to hang onto it. They as rare as a pair of clean socks around a bunkhouse, haw haw."

Vangie saw that Gabe's beetled glance was fixed on the gateway behind them. It was open and a wagon came in—DORALDO MINE, SONORA—drawn by the customary dozens of mules and surrounded by the customary outriders, who looked like displaced members of Genghis Khan's palace guard. The knot of tourists followed the guide toward the front door but Gabe hung back, watching the wagon as it went along the side of the main building and stopped by a loading platform where uniformed sentries hulked.

She tugged at Gabe's sleeve. "Come on."

"In a minute. In a minute." He was chewing on an unlit cigar, watching as attentively as a lecher watching a nun disrobe. The muleskinner had unhitched the wheel team and half a dozen of the guards were shoving on the wagon tongue to push it back against the loading platform, where more men began to unload the boxes of gold onto a cart.

It looked like the kind of wheeled dumpcart they used in mineshafts—a hand-push cart mounted on railroad wheels. From this angle Vangie couldn't see any rails, but she assumed they must be there, leading back into the building.

"Come *on*," she whispered insistently and dragged him quickly to the front door, through which the tourists were disappearing. She glanced over her shoulder and saw both gate guards scowling in their direction. She hurried Gabe inside.

"Now the annual production of the mines here in California," the guide was intoning, "is in the vicinity of twenny million dollars. Now folks, that's just a whole lot of dollars. Why if you took twenny million dollars in one-dollar greenjackets, it would stretch from here to—well I don't rightly re-collect exactly where, maybe Chicago, but it'd reach pret' near two thousand miles. And that's a long way to walk laying greenjacket bills end to end just to prove a stupid point, haw haw. Now the way the United States Mint operates here, we get shipments of clean-smelted gold ingots in from the mines just about every day, but what we do, we wait till we've got anywheres from one to two million dollars worth of gold to strike before we start up the presses, which I'm just about to show you on over here. So anyhow, three-four times a year we run off a stamping, and every year or two we got to change the mold-plates. Course we could keep the presses running all the time, stamp out coins every day from every little ship-ment, but that'd be a lot more costly and your Gov'ment is lookin' out for your interests by operating in the most eco-nomical way. I guess all us citizens apprayshate that, haw haw."

Vangie looked with approval on the great number of armed guards they passed in the hallways. Everywhere you turned, there was a man in uniform with a gun and a grim expression.

Each time she spotted another guard, she plucked at Gabe's sleeve to make sure he noticed. He kept nodding impatiently and shaking her off.

The guide took them into the pressroom and spent the longest eight minutes she'd ever experienced describing, in more detail than anybody wanted to hear, the process of melt-ing ingots, pouring them into the molds, transferring the blank new discs onto the presses, and stamping the sides. Gabe kept shifting restively from foot to foot and sweeping the ceiling with his glance.

It wasn't really a huge building but the number of turnings and corridors made it seem endless. The bored, rote intona-tions of the guide's voice kept ringing in stone-bounced echoes and Vangie became eager to get out of this place. It had all the homey comfortable warmth of a Mexican vampire cave, one of which she had once seen. One was too many.

They turned yet another corner. "And this here," the guide announced, "is where the gold comes in from the mines. Now you folks are most fortunate this mornin' because we actually have a shipment coming in right now as you can see. Now mind you don't get run over, haw—that little cart's pretty durned heavy, you better believe me, haw haw."

The handcart was coming along the rails, carrying the boxed gold down a wide corridor. At the far end was the loading platform they'd seen from outside. The rails crossed in front of them and went into another room.

Two guys were pushing the handcart and half a dozen guards walked along beside it. As they passed the tourist group they began to turn, so that finally most of them were walking backwards. One of them backed right into the door-jamb and some of the tourists snickered. The guard got very red in the face and ducked out of sight through the doorway, but it quickly became clear that wouldn't save him because the guide was leading the party right in through the same door, following him.

"Now this here's the anteroom to our storage vault," the guide told them. "Can everybody see back there?"

The people in back murmured that they could see. Not that it mattered to Vangie, since she and Gabe were no longer among the people at the back. From hanging around at the very rear of the group all through the first part of the tour, Gabe had now insisted on shoving his way up to the very front. And Vangie knew why; that damned vault was calling to him with its siren song, all about gold.

The anteroom was just an empty square space surrounded by walls without windows. The tracks went on through and out another doorway on the opposite side; the gold shipment with all its guards was just leaving the anteroom as the tour group filed in.

The guide waited till everybody was in before going on with his spiel. "Now," he said, "we ain't allowed past this point, so I'll just let each of you come over here close to the door and peek past my shoulder if you'd like to see the vault. It's right through here, this doorway. Now mind you, not too close—these here boys get right nervous if they see anybody leanin' too passionately toward that gold inside, haw haw."

Gabe was the first to step forward and finally Vangie had to drag him aside to let the other people have a look. She herself got only a glimpse into the vault.

It didn't look extraordinary. Just a ten-by-ten room with a big steel door at the far end of it, into which ran the handcart rails. The guards were unloading the boxes and stacking them on shelves inside the vault at the far side of the room. The big steel door was open. A guard now came across from the steel door and slammed shut an open-grille door of steel bars, like a jail cell door, of which Vangie had seen one or two in her time. It didn't block anyone's view, but the steel bars looked about three inches thick. It was obvious nobody was going to open that door without a key and a lot of friends.

She began to feel a little better about things. Gabe's idea was clearly impossible after all.

"Now this here barred door is closed and locked virtually at all times, folks, except when there's a cart going through, as you just seen. And of course at these times we keep a minimum force of twenny armed guards in these two rooms, not to mention all the guards you saw around the rest of the Mint. So you can rest assured your money's safe, haw haw. Nobody's ever tried to rob the United States Mint, of course —nobody's ever been stupid enough to try. I reckon someday somebody will, but you probably won't even read about it in the papers, because whatever they do they ain't gonna get anywheres near your Gov'ment's gold."

Vangie was absolutely positive the guide had said that strictly for Gabe's benefit. But Gabe was smiling faintly as if his head were filled with pleasant faraway visions. He didn't seem to be listening to the guide any more. He was looking up at the corners of the anteroom, just under the ceiling. Vangie looked up that way, but she couldn't see anything but walls and ceiling.

The guide reached over to touch the heavy steel panel beside the barred door. "And this here solid steel door—this is armor plate, by the way—this is kept closed and locked at all times except visiting hours."

Gabe obviously wasn't listening at all any more. His glance swiveled back from the vault room, and Vangie, following the direction of his gaze, didn't see anything that looked important. He was just looking out the corridor toward the loading platform at the far end.

It was all one long straight line, she noticed. From the loading platform the rails came straight through the building, through the anteroom, and right into the vault.

The guide took them out through the office-lined corridors that led to the front door. There seemed to be a guard at every turning.

By the time they got out to the main gate, Vangie was feeling highly relieved. It was obviously impossible to crack this place. Now Gabe would have to give up the idea completely.

Gabe nodded judiciously as they walked out through the gate. "Well," he said, "that shouldn't be too tough."

He didn't seem to notice the look Vangie gave him.

The street led directly downhill from the Mint's main gate to the Bay, which spread out before them in all its sunlit glory. They strolled down toward the center of the city, Gabe off in unguessable plans and speculations, Vangie fretting and fuming and wondering just how serious Gabe was about putting his head into this particular noose.

A block or two from the Mint they passed a policeman and

Vangie recognized him as Officer McCorkle, with his red hair sticking out from under his bobby helmet as though it were a wig. He was the one who'd arrested that fellow in the Golden Rule that time, the fellow who'd tried to shoot Ittzy Herz.

Apparently Officer McCorkle thought he recognized Vangie and Gabe as well. He gave them both a searching glance as they passed him by, and when she looked back at him he had taken an enormous notebook from his hip pocket and was flipping through the pages. He selected one, took a stub of pencil from his shirt pocket, wetted it on his tongue preparatory to taking notes, and glanced again toward Vangie and Gabe.

Vangie guiltily faced front. Beside her, Gabe walked blissfully along, unaware of everything. But she could practically *feel* that pencil writing away on the back of her head.

He's just waiting for us to get in trouble, Vangie thought. It was obvious that McCorkle had his eye on them. Should she say something to Gabe? No, he'd just think she was trying to scare him out of planning this Mint robbery.

Troubled, oppressed, but for the moment keeping her own counsel, Vangie walked along beside her man.

12

Francis' pleasure in the day was about to be spoiled. "I don't understand," he complained, "why you want to go out to that awful place."

Gabe said, "It's just a nice ride in the country, think of it that way."

"A ride into disaster, you mean." Francis was sulky because the cancan shows were still forcibly shut down and none of his other potential projects had come through—the dress boutique, for instance, or the tea shoppe.

Vangie said, "Oh, come on, Francis, it'll be fun. Fresh air and sunshine."

Feeling betrayed by the girl, Francis said to her, "Why, I thought you didn't approve of all this."

"I don't," she said. "But I wouldn't pass up a beautiful day in the country. Besides, you don't care about that old mine anyway."

He did, in fact, he minded terribly, but he only sighed and said, "Oh, very well. If we must, we must."

They were walking along through a light fog, of a pearly thinness so translucent that it hardly counted as a fog at all in San Franciscan terms. As they strolled down Front Street to Hansen's Livery, the fog rolled in more heavily from the Bay, entirely obscuring the world in white for thirty seconds or so, then whisking itself away like smoke in a magic act, revealing—a corral full of nags for rent.

Francis, feeling a bit better now that he'd resigned himself to visiting the mine of his undoing, said, "My, that is a stirring sight, isn't it?"

"I look best on a black horse," Vangie said.

"Yes, you're right," Francis told her. "That would go with your coloring."

Gabe said, "I look best in a buggy, so that's what we'll get."

Pouting, Vangie said, "But I want to *ride*."

Gabe said, "Vangie, I've never been on top of a horse in my life and I'm not about to start now."

Vangie gave him a contemptuous stare. "You are a dude, aren't you?"

"Horses are for pulling things," Gabe said. "I don't sit on them, and they don't sit on me."

"Tenderfoot."

"Better a tender foot," Gabe told her. "We'll take a buggy. Of course, if you want, you can stay here in town."

Francis, seeing a battle brewing, made an attempt to soothe it. "Oh, really," he said, "sometimes a victoria can be fun. The breeze in one's face, a pleasant ride. Don't you think so, Vangie?"

Vangie looked doubtful and mutinous. She seemed to be working out the exact phrasing of a statement that Francis was sure he didn't want to hear, so he hurried on, saying, "Come on, dear, we'll see if they have something interesting. Something really ladylike and nice."

Vangie permitted herself to be led away by Francis, who took her around the side of the corral to where a number of bedraggled buggies and gigs were lined up along a muddy stretch beside a railed fence. Forcing himself to be light-hearted in the teeth of all this depressing naturalism, Francis said, "Well, do you see anything you like?"

She turned her head slowly and gave him a look.

Before Francis could decide what to do or say next, the stable hostler came gimping over. A crabbed man of indeterminate age, in filthy clothes, he gave the appearance that his entire body was in a permanent squint. "Ah, my good man," Francis said inaccurately. "We were hoping to rent a victoria for the day."

"And how about a Myrtle for tonight?" The hostler giggled, wheezed and hugged himself until he noticed Vangie looking at him; then he got surly and just stood there, squinting over his whole body. "Got no victoria," he said, and spat something brown into the mud.

"What *do* you have?" Francis asked. Years ago, he'd decided the only way to survive in this life was to pretend that everybody else was also civilized, no matter what they did. Sometimes the pretence was harder to maintain than at other times.

"What you see right there in front of you," the hostler said, and jabbed a thumb at the line of wagons along the fence.

Gabe joined them then and pointed to one of the wagons. "What's that?" he said.

Everybody looked at him. Nobody could figure out what question he was asking. Doubtfully, the hostler said, "It's for rent."

"I know. What's it called?"

The hostler squinted more than ever. "You havin' fun with me?"

Francis said gently, "Gabe, you're such a city person."

"Yeah, I've noticed that about me."

"It's called a buckboard."

"We could all three sit up on front there, couldn't we?"

"Yes, of course," Francis said. He frowned toward Vangie, wondering if she would accept a buckboard after he'd built her up to anticipate a much more elegant victoria. But her mulish expression hadn't changed at all, either for the better or the worse. "A buckboard," Francis said again, trying to sound enthusiastic. "Why, it might be a lot of fun at that."

"It'll get us there," Gabe said, and turned to deal with the hostler.

Once a swaybacked roan with a sty in its off eye had been attached to the buckboard and the squinting hostler had been dealt with in a financial way, Francis, Gabe and Vangie crowded together up onto the seat. Gabe said, "Okay. Who drives?"

Francis looked at him in astonishment. "Can't you?"

"I was never more than two blocks from the trolley line the first twenty-five years of my life," Gabe said. "What would I be doing driving one of these things?"

Francis swallowed. "Well," he said, "I must confess I've always considered myself too butterfingered to want to——"

"Oh, give me those," Vangie said in disgust, picking up the reins. "HYAAAAAAHHH!" she told the roan. "Giddap!"

The wagon bolted away with a jerk that almost flipped Francis off the seat.

The August sun on the Peninsula was hot, far too hot. Francis dragged his limp lace handkerchief over his face and regretted the moment of weakness in which he'd agreed to come out here. "I've only been to this awful hole in the ground twice in my life," he said. "I'm not sure I can find it again."

"Oh, you'll find it," Gabe said. Between them, Vangie held the reins and watched the roan and occasionally glanced around at the barren countryside. Her bad temper seemed to have worked itself out on the act of driving, much to Francis' relief, and though there hadn't been that much conversation on the ride out at least they'd all been friendly to one another.

But now there was the problem of finding the supposed mine. "But what if I can't find it?" Francis asked. "I'd hate to have brought us all out here for nothing."

"You'll find it," Gabe told him, "because we're gonna stay out here and look for it until you do."

The sun instantly became ten degrees hotter. "Uh," Francis said, and mopped his brow, and looked around harder for something to recognize.

They passed a place where some hopeful hardrocker had tried to strike it rich. Vangie said, "I didn't know anyone ever found any gold on the Peninsula. I thought it was all in the mountains across the Bay."

"Well they did find a few traces, apparently," Francis said. "But to my chagrin that's all they were. Traces."

"But there's a tunnel," Gabe said.

"Yes."

"Well that's all we need."

"For what?" Vangie asked.

"Just an idea I have," he said.

"It's still that craziness about the Mint, isn't it?"

"Could be," Gabe said easily. "What's wrong with that?"

"Only one thing," she said. "If you try anything anywhere *near* that Mint they'll catch you. If they don't kill you on the spot, they'll put you away somewhere until you've got a long grey beard. Or maybe they'll just fall all over you—ten or fifteen of those guards we saw up there—and by the time they get finished with you, your skin won't be worth tanning. *That's* what's wrong."

"Well," Gabe replied obscurely, "chicken today, feathers tomorrow." And he grinned at her.

It was all steep hills down the spine of the Peninsula here, stands of pine and redwood among the rocks. As they prowled farther into the morning and into the noon sun, Francis drooped lower and lower in the seat. He was afraid he'd missed the turnoff, and he didn't doubt that Gabe had meant what he'd said about keeping him out here until he found the mine. It looked like it was going to be a long dry spell——No. There it was, right ahead. He straightened up. "That little dirt track. Turn off the road there."

Vangie swung the buckboard expertly into the twin ruts and they went jouncing up into the trees. It was cool here in the shade and Francis began to feel somewhat less suicidal. "Just ahead now, on the left. There'll be another fork and we take the left one."

"Well I told you not to expect anything," he said defensively.

The place was nothing but a wide spot in the rocks and a man-sized hole in the hillside. The tunnel disappeared back into the mountain. Claim stakes stood at the corners of the claim; the previous owners' names had been scratched out and FRANCIS CALHOUN was printed conspicuously on each stake.

Gabe stood backed against a rock, thumbs hooked in his pockets, scowling, chewing a cigar, while Vangie fashioned a torch out of a broken branch and some twigs and grass. When she handed it to Gabe she smiled with mock-sweetness but Gabe ignored it, ducked into the tunnel, and lit the torch.

It had been a long and bumpy ride, coming out. "Excuse me," Francis said to Vangie and went off into the woods to commune with Nature.

When he returned he found Gabe and Vangie wrapped around each other as if they were the only survivors of a volcanic eruption. Francis rolled his eyes upward and said, by way of announcing his presence, "Have you two met?"

They broke apart, both showing their embarrassment in the

hue of their cheeks. Gabe grumbled something and went prowling back into the mine. Vangie fidgeted with her hair; Francis tipped his shoulder against the buckboard and folded his arms across his chest. "Well?"

She shrugged, accepting no blame. "He likes the place."

"He does?"

"Francis, don't ask me. I don't know any more than you do."

"Well he does seem sure of himself, doesn't he. But frankly I was a little worried right from the start. I mean, he said he wanted *my* help. Now that does make one a bit dubious of his judgment, doesn't it? I mean, what do you suppose he wants me to do for him? Maim and disfigure people and kill the ones he doesn't like?"

"Well I imagine that's not exactly what he has in mind. Though God knows what he does have in his mind." She moved closer and dropped her voice to a confidential half whisper. "Francis, what was he like in the old days?"

"Gabe? You mean back in New York? Oh, he was about the same. He always talked a bigger brand of meanness than he owned. I mean, he's deliciously rough on the outside, isn't he, but underneath he's really very kind."

"Does he have a girl back there?"

"He usually did. I don't know about now. I hadn't seen him in years and years, you know."

She looked pensively toward the tunnel. "I don't know if I could like New York," she said.

Surprise on surprise. Francis looked at her and said, "Why on earth should you ever go there?"

She shrugged again, looking more like a lost orphan than usual. "I don't know," she said. "Gabe keeps saying he's going back there just as soon as he gets enough money."

"Back to New York? Whatever for?"

"He says it's the only place to live."

· *101* ·

Francis' own memories of the Big Apple were less delicious. "After seeing San Francisco?" he said, astonished.

"He says San Francisco is a lumpy Newark."

"And you'd actually go with him?"

"I don't know," she said. Her brow was as furrowed as the hillside. "I wouldn't want to, but I guess if he asked me I'd go, yes."

"Oh, I can't lose you both," Francis said. "We'll just have to convince Gabe to change his mind."

She looked hopeful. "Do you think we can?"

"We can only try."

She clasped his hand in both of hers. "Francis," she said, "I'm glad you're on my side."

His heart full, Francis told her the simple truth: "You're my dearest friends," he said.

13

Gabe stood outside the Mint.

He had been standing there for hours in the fog, watching.

About eleven in the morning the fog burned off. He shifted his weight to the other foot.

A little past noon Vangie brought him his lunch in a paper bag. He ate mechanically, watching the Mint, totally self-absorbed.

At one-fifteen there was an alarm of bells, and Gabe stepped back into a doorway. Fire horses careened into the street, and the great red fire engine went thundering through the city.

It went downstreet toward the waterfront. Up over the lower rise and then on toward Pacific Street. From his hilltop vantage point Gabe watched narrowly, thoughtfully.

At half-past three he was still standing there when he saw McCorkle, the tall red-haired cop, staring at him dubiously from across the street. McCorkle took a huge notebook out of his hip pocket, jotted something down, and then went on around the corner out of sight.

At five Gabe headed downhill.

Five-oh-three, another fire alarm. He got off the street. The fire-engine went past with an earsplitting noise—flash of white, flash of red.

Down below near the foot of the hill, two figures stood out in isolated silhouette because they were the only two people still on the street. Gabe narrowed his eyes to pierce the five-block downhill distance. Finally he recognized the two figures.

It was Ittzy Herz's mother dragging Ittzy across the street by the ear.

Mme. Herz was talking. Evidently she was talking so loudly that she didn't hear the fire engine.

It filled Gabe's vision, blocking Mme. and Ittzy from his view. The fire engine was obviously going to trample them both.

But then the dust began to settle in the engine's wake and Ittzy and his mother were still walking across the street, unperturbed; Mrs. Herz continued to drag Ittzy by the ear and yell at him.

Gabe shook his head in renewed amazement and went on down to the Golden Rule Saloon.

Inside, Vangie and Francis were at the usual table—the one just big enough for three glasses and six elbows. Gabe threaded a path to them and sat.

They were having coffee and Francis was complaining about it. "They brew it up six weeks in advance and pour some molasses in and, my dears, they simply let it *sit*. And then they drop a horse-shoe into it, and if the horse-shoe sinks the coffee isn't strong enough."

Gabe adjusted his elbows on the table. "What do you expect from this burg? Real coffee?"

Vangie put on her arch look. "And just what's wrong with this *burg*?"

"It's too far from New York."

"Will you forget New York?"

"No."

Vangie turned to Francis, who was touching the surface of his coffee with a doubting fingertip. "Francis," she said, "you used to live in New York. You like San Francisco better, don't you?"

Francis looked up. "Well, I do, yes, I suppose," he said. He licked coffee from his fingertip, made a face, and gave Gabe a quick worried look. His brow furrowed in his obvious effort to please everybody. "But different people are, uh, well, different. Gabe might rather——"

"Gabe," Vangie interrupted fiercely, "could do just fine in San Francisco. He could make a million dollars here."

"Yeah," Gabe said. "That's just what I'm going to do. I want to talk to you about that, Francis."

But Vangie wouldn't let the conversation be changed. "This is a city of *great* opportunity," she said, leaning closer to Gabe and holding tight to his forearm on the table. "A man with your brains, Gabe, why, you could *own* this city if you wanted."

"I don't want."

"But——"

Gabe made one more effort to get his point across. "The city I want to own," he said, "is New York. All I want from this burg is enough cash money so I can go back to New York in style."

Francis said, "Why did Twill throw—that is, why did you have to leave?"

"Aagh," Gabe said in disgust, "the fat son of a bitch said the neighborhood needed a little shaking up. Said they were forgetting who the boss was, some of them. So I had to go out and shake things up a little. Or down."

"Down?" Vangie said.

"I shook somebody down. A pushcart peddler. I mean, you got to keep these people in their places, otherwise they start thinking maybe you're not as tough as you say you are."

Francis said, "So you shook down a pushcart peddler. What did you do to him?"

"Hardly a thing. I just looked fierce and took a little kickback from him for allowing him the privilege of working on Twill's turf."

"Well what went wrong then?"

Gabe threw up his hands. "How was I to know he was the wrong peddler to push? How was I to know his nephew was one of Twill's ward bosses? The guy had no right pushing a cart. I mean if he was *my* dear old uncle and *I* was the ward boss, would *I* let him push a crummy cart around the streets? I ask you."

"And so this ward boss complained to Twill?"

"Complained? I guess maybe he complained. He wanted them to dump me off a pier."

"But one gathers they didn't."

Gabe let his lip curl. "This ward boss wasn't as high as me on the neighborhood ladder."

"Then why'd Twill listen to him at all?"

"Because the ward boss's sister is Twill's mother-in-law." Gabe shuddered. "*Mother*-in-law." He turned swiftly to Vangie. "Listen, you haven't got a mother hidden out somewhere around here, have you? Because if you do, the whole——"

"She died when I was nine," Vangie said.

Gabe gulped. "Oh, hey, listen Vangie, I'm sorry, I didn't mean—I just got kind of carried away. I mean——"

"Never mind. It's all right." She patted his hand. Then she stiffened. "What about *your* mother?"

He darkened immediately. "Are you trying to besmirch my good mother's sainted memory?"

"I'm sure I'd have loved her," Vangie said soothingly. "She *has*—passed on, then?"

"Yeah," he grunted. Then he gave her a suspicious look, but she was smiling guilelessly.

Francis said, "So Twill told you to leave town because his mother-in-law was angry with you."

"Yeah." Gabe made a fist. "It wouldn't have happened if I hadn't been broke at the time."

Vangie said, "Why not?"

Gabe glowered at the tabletop. "Listen, you can buy a lot of smiles with money. If I'd only had a few thousand dollars to grease the right people I'd still be running that neighborhood. Instead of out here in the sticks. But I'm gonna get enough money out of this burg to fix all that. A man with a million dollars doesn't *have* enemies. Not even mother-in-law enemies."

Francis said, "A *million* dollars?"

"What do you think they keep up there at the Mint? Chicken feed?"

"You don't really think you can. . . . The Mint?"

Gabe leaned forward earnestly. "Kid, you know me from the old days. Now if Gabe Beauchamps says he's going to do a thing, does he do it?"

Francis beamed. "He does. He certainly does."

Vangie turned angrily on Francis. "You—double-crosser!"

"What?"

"What do you mean agreeing with him? You can't possibly agree with him. Nobody on *earth* could rob the United States Mint."

"Well, I don't know, Vangie," Francis said. He was in the middle again. "If anybody could do it," he said, "I guess Gabe would be the one."

"But nobody *can*," she insisted.

Gabe had heard enough of this. "I can," he growled.

Francis looked from Vangie to Gabe, from Gabe to Vangie, and from Vangie to Gabe again. His mouth opened a few times, but he didn't say anything.

Gabe finally took the poor fish off the hook. "Don't worry about it, Francis," he said. "Vangie just feels protective toward me, that's all."

"I suppose that's it," Francis said, giving them both a shaky grin.

"Though I don't know why I should," Vangie said, glowering at the table at large.

Gabe grinned at her. She was a feisty little thing and that was a lot of her charm. He could put up with a certain amount of disagreement, just so she didn't overdo it. "That's okay, honey," he said. "You make me think things over an extra time, and that's good."

"It would be," she said, "if it would ever change your mind."

He grinned again, patted her hand, and turned back to Francis. "I told you," he said, "there's room in this for you, if you want in."

Francis looked interested. "Do you know how you're going to do it?"

"I've got my idea pretty well worked out," Gabe said.

Vangie said, "Francis, do you want to go to jail?"

Which put Francis in the middle again. "Well," he said, and moved his hands around.

This time he was saved by a tremendous crash. Gabe was almost inured to spectacular noises around here by now but this one was so close it almost knocked him off his chair. He whipped around, ready to duck, run, or fight, and at first saw nothing but a thick cloud of dust in the middle of the saloon. But then he made out what had happened.

It was the main chandelier, which must have weighed half a ton, all heavy crystal and pewter. It had fallen to the floor as though going to China the quick way. Smoke, dust, and debris filled the air in a big billowing cloud; the echoes of the crash rang back and forth like mission bells in a thunderstorm.

And out of the cloud came Ittzy Herz, unruffled, dusting himself off.

"Him," Gabe said. "I want *him* in the gang."

14

Ittzy was checking to make sure he'd brushed all the plaster dust off himself when someone touched his arm. He thought at first it was just another prospector hoping for good luck, but it was Vangie Kemp.

"Hi, Ittzy."

"Why, uh, hi, uh, Miss, uh, Kemp."

He wished he didn't get tongue-tied around pretty girls. It was really embarrassing.

"Come on over to the table," she said. Her smile almost paralyzed him, but he managed to shuffle over to the table in her wake.

"Ittzy, this is Gabe Beauchamps, and that's Francis Calhoun. We wondered if we could talk to you for a minute."

Ittzy shook hands with the two fellows and pulled out the chair Vangie indicated.

Vangie said, "You ran away from your mother again, huh?"

"I'm thirty-four years old," Ittzy said. "I want to have a life of my own."

The tough-looking one, Gabe, stared at him in awe. "You're *thirty-four years old?*"

"Well, I know I look a little younger."

"You look goddam nineteen."

Vangie explained, "It's because he never worries."

"But I got to thinking this morning," Ittzy said. "I mean, the Book says I get threescore and ten, and next month's my birthday. You know what that means?"

"What does that mean?" Francis Calhoun asked.

Ittzy wasn't sure about the look this Calhoun fellow was giving him. If he didn't know better he'd think it was jealousy. But that couldn't be. He said, "Well, it means I've used up half my time next month. You know? Thirty-five gone, thirty-five to go. I mean, it's time I got out on my own."

"It sure is," Gabe Beauchamps said. "Vangie told me about your problem, Ittzy, and she thinks you're a fine fellow. It occurred to us we had something you might just consider a possibility right along those same lines, so we thought we'd let you in on it."

This Gabe fellow certainly was talking fast. Ittzy said, "You are?" And looked at Vangie. "You, uh, uh, are?"

"What you need," Gabe Beauchamps said, "is financial independence. What I mean to say is money of your own."

Ittzy had never heard anybody talk so fast in his life. He looked at Vangie, "Uh, uh?"

Gabe was leaning toward him, elbows on the table, gesticulating to emphasize his words. "If the farthest your finances will take you is the other side of the Bay, how can you ever get away from your mother's emporium? No, my friend, I have exactly the prescription you need right here. And what it is, what you need, is money. *Big* money."

Ittzy frowned. He certainly did like Vangie. And he had nothing against her friends. But this was beginning to sound familiar. "I don't want to go prospecting," he said.

"Huh?"

Francis Calhoun looked alarmed. "*Prospecting?*"

Ittzy said, "People always want me to go prospecting with them. I *hate* prospecting."

Gabe was grinning from ear to ear. "My friend those are exactly my sentiments, isn't that a coincidence? I mean to say, I couldn't agree with you more, you're exactly one-hundred-percent entirely right. Even a rinky-dink town like this is better than slogging around in all the rain and mud out in the sticks there. Yes sir, you are absolutely right."

"You mean you don't want to go looking for gold?"

"Well now, I wouldn't go exactly that far. We are looking for gold, yes indeed."

Ittzy was disappointed. He began to push his chair back. "I'm sorry. I'm just not interested in prospecting."

Gabe touched his arm. "Even if you don't have to leave San Francisco to do it?"

Ittzy frowned. "There isn't any gold in San Francisco," he said.

Gabe grinned and winked, and leaned back to hook his thumbs in his vest pockets. "Well, yes, there is," he said. "As a matter of fact, there is."

Ittzy looked at Vangie, but she was looking at him and that only made it more difficult to think. "Uh," he said, for no reason, and looked back at Gabe. "Where is it?" he asked.

Gabe gestured toward the outside world, nodding in that direction. "Up at the top of the hill there," he said. "Up at the Mint."

Blinking, Ittzy said, "Up at the Mint?"

"You're right," Gabe told him.

"I am?"

Vangie said, "Ittzy, Gabe means to *steal* the gold from the Mint."

"Oh, *steal!*" Ittzy beamed and nodded; now he understood. He knew what stealing was. It was merely a continuation of

· *111* ·

merchandising by other means. "Well now, that's much better."

Vangie stared at him. "You mean you'd *do* it?"

Gabe gave her a sharp glance. "Why shouldn't he? Ittzy's a grown man. He's thirty-four years old. He doesn't have a thing in the world to be afraid of, do you Ittzy?"

"Nothing except my Mama."

"Exactly. And with that gold you could be safe from your Mama for ever and ever."

"Why I guess I really could, couldn't I?"

"Why of course you could, my friend. Of *course* you could." Gabe leaned forward very close to him. "You with us?"

Ittzy looked around at the three friendly faces. So much better than the back room of the shop and the staring eyes at the peephole.

"I'm with you," he said.

15

Gabe felt proud of himself. It was the first con spiel he'd essayed since he'd left New York, and he'd been afraid he might be getting a little rusty. But it had worked with Ittzy and he felt a whole lot more confident now.

"The next thing we need," he said, "is a boat."

Francis said, "A boat? What kind of boat?"

"A big one. Maybe a ship."

Vangie gawked at him. "You're going on a *ship?*"

"For a million dollars I'm willing to throw up a little."

"I swear I never thought I'd see the day."

"Well, it's the only way. I've thought and thought, but there's no other answer. Look, we have to get the stuff out of San Francisco. That means either a boat or a wagon. There's only one wagon road—down the Peninsula—and they could telegraph ahead and cut us off."

Vangie said, "Couldn't you cut the telegraph wire?"

Gabe frowned at her. "But what if there was an emergency and somebody had to telegraph for a doctor or something? I mean, you can't just go around cutting Western Union wires all over the place. Somebody could get hurt."

Francis said, "Besides, with a wagonload of gold you wouldn't be able to go terribly fast, dear. They'd overtake us in just *no* time on horseback."

Gabe said, "It's gotta be a ship," and waited.

Francis said, "I'm sorry, old cock, I'm afraid I don't know anyone with a ship."

"I know somebody," said Ittzy.

They all looked at him. Gabe said, "Who?"

"Flagway," Ittzy said. "His name's Captain Flagway. He has a ship."

"What does he do with it?"

"Nothing. His crew jumped ship and ran away to the gold fields."

Vangie said, "He could have hired Roscoe's crimpers to get him a new crew."

"He won't do that. He says it's wrong, I don't know why."

Gabe said, "Does he need money, by any chance?"

"He sure does," Ittzy said.

Gabe stood up. "Well, the only thing we'll get if we wait around here is whiskers. Let's go see this guy."

Along the waterfront Gabe kept his eyes averted from the Bay side of the street. In New York you could live thirty years without once seeing a ship. You could completely ignore the fact that Manhattan was even an island. But in San Francisco you could hardly look across the street without being confronted by roiling water and heaving ships.

Ittzy led them to a bedraggled sailing ship with several masts. Gabe wouldn't know a clipper from a dinghy, but this one looked plenty big enough, whatever make and model it was.

Whether it would go more than five miles without sinking was another question. It seemed ready to disintegrate at a moment's notice. Most of the paint was worn off and he wood beneath was splintery and rotten. The big mast in the middle of the ship was slightly off kilter and looked about to fall over. The entire vessel appeared to be in an advanced state of dilapidated decay.

It was tied up at an equally rotten pier, half a mile below the main waterfront. The dock area around here consisted mainly of abandoned shacks and windowless warehouses.

Gabe was beginning to feel queasy before they even stepped onto the dock, but he took a deep breath and persevered.

The ship's name was painted across the stern in faded red letters. *San Andreas.* Above that a flag hung from a staff canted vertiginously over the stern. Gabe didn't recognize the colors. "What country's that?"

Ittzy said, "Paraguay."

"Paraguay?"

"It's a country in South America," Vangie said.

Francis was frowning. "Something's decidedly fishy about that."

"You can say that again," Gabe said, wrinkling his nostrils.

"No, I don't mean that, old cock. The thing is, you see, Paraguay's a landlocked country. No seacoast. No ports."

It sounded like Heaven to Gabe.

Ittzy said, "Well they do have a flag. That's it right there."

"But how can they have ships if they haven't got any harbors?" Vangie asked.

Nobody seemed to have an answer for that. They headed for the gangplank that came down from the side of the boat to the dock. Gabe stopped at the foot of the plank. "I think I'll wait here. You go aboard and bring him out, and we'll take him somewhere for a drink."

Vangie said, sympathetically, "Is it getting to you?"

"I'll be all right," Gabe said. "As long as I don't have to talk about it."

"We'll be right back," she said.

"That's fine," he said, and turned purposefully away as Vangie, Francis and Ittzy went up the undulating gangplank and on board the ship.

Gabe waited with his back to the sea, fixing his eyes on the hills inland. He could still hear the sickening slap and gulp of the water against the pilings and the ship, but he bore up stoically until the others finally returned.

"Nobody's on board," Vangie said.

Ittzy said, "He must be around somewhere. He never goes far."

"Well, let's find him, then," Gabe said.

They walked off the pier and turned up the street toward town. Things were very quiet and deserted down in this neighborhood.

As they passed an alley, Gabe glanced into it and saw an unhappy gentleman in semi-nautical attire, engaged in a dispute with two burly guys. Another look and Gabe realized that they were Roscoe and his partner, the crimpers. They were approaching the nautical gentleman from opposite sides with rope manacles.

"Help!" the gentleman cried. "Oh, *do* help!"

Ittzy shouted, "That's Captain Flagway!"

"Ho, ho," Gabe said.

He headed into the alley, reaching for his knuckle-duster with one hand and the loaded whisky-flask with the other. As he approached Roscoe's identity was confirmed, if it needed confirming, by the gamy odor that infused the alleyway.

Roscoe and the other guy squared off to meet his approach when from behind him he heard Francis say, loud and clear, "Roscoe, you put that man down this minute!"

It made Roscoe look past Gabe. Suddenly he became very embarrassed. He released Captain Flagway at once, looked at his partner, and turned away with a disgusted look, fading back into the narrow passages between the warehouses. His baffled partner hesitated a second, then followed.

Gabe looked over his shoulder in bewilderment at Francis, who was looking after the attempted crimpers with a very stern expression on his face, like a fussy housewife finding muddy footprints in the parlor.

Gabe shook his head and turned back to Captain Flagway, who had staggered to the nearest wall and was leaning against it, mopping his brow. "Oh, thank you, dear friends," he said.

"Any time," said Gabe.

"I kept telling them," Captain Flagway said, "that I was captain, not crew, but they wouldn't listen."

Ittzy, coming forward, said, "Are you all right, Captain Flagway?"

The captain looked up in surprise. "Ittzy? Is that you?"

"We've been looking for you," Ittzy said. "These are some friends of mine. Uh, Vangie, uh, Kemp. And Gabe Beauchamps. And Francis Calhoun."

"I am delighted to meet you all," said the captain. "I assure you I'm delighted."

Francis said priggishly, "That Roscoe is an absolute menace. He's going to get himself in a great deal of trouble someday."

Gabe said to the captain, "I hear you've been stuck in this port for a while."

The captain nodded, his expression becoming mournful. "Three years," he said. "Three years and two months, to be exact."

"It must be tough on you," Gabe said.

"Mine," the captain said, "is a long sad story."

Gabe took him by the arm. "We'll buy you a drink," he said, "and you can tell it."

16

Captain Flagway reached for his drink. "My story began in Baltimore," he said, "where I was a clerk in my Daddy's apothecary shop. One night on Eager Street I was approached by two men not unlike the two you kind people just rescued me from. Their intent was, I daresay, the same—to impress me into the crew of an understaffed steamer. I fear that night in Baltimore there were no Good Samaritans such as yourselves to come to my aid in my moment of distress. And so my saga of despair began. I *was* in fact impressed and found myself aboard the *Magna Carta*, a British vessel transporting cotton to Liverpool."

He drank. "I had hoped to jump ship on its return to Baltimore—I knew Daddy would be worried. Unfortunately, however, the *Magna Carta*'s next consignment was a cargo of cotton loincloths billed to Lagos, which is of course in Africa.

"On the way I had an altercation with bos'un and found it discretionary to leave the ship in Lagos. I had several adventuresome tribulations before signing on a passing French freighter called *Egalité*, anticipating returning to Europe and there, surely, finding another ship bound for the States."

He drank. "Unfortunately, however, *Egalité*'s consignment was a cargo of indentured servants billed to the Caribbean, whence she took rum to Brazil. In Rio de Janeiro I once again switched vessels, and found myself on a ship carrying coffee to the Azores. Surely, I felt, somewhere in the Lord's vast sea there must be a ship heading for the States. Unfortunately however, I did not encounter such, and then at last, in South America once again, I boarded an Argentine clipper, the *San Andreas*, which was bound for San Diego with a cargo of sandals and sangria."

He drank. "There were at that time approximately fourteen separate and distinct wars being carried on simultaneously throughout South America, with each nation participating in five or six alliances and two or three of the wars. Under those conditions it was not unnatural that privateers should be numerous and active, of course, and one constantly risked being accosted at sea by such ruffians—they were everywhere, always claiming ships for this or that country.

"We succeeded in beating round the Horn in a savage maelstrom of wind, snow and hurtling ice, but in our voyage northward along the Pacific coast we were unfortunately discovered by a roaming man-of-war. It was a sad affair I can assure you. We were captured by Venezuelan freebooters. They, in turn, were taken by Chilean privateers. Next we were overwhelmed by elements of the Ecuadorian Navy. We then headed in toward shore but were ambushed by Colombian commandeers who, like the rest, took the ship as a prize of war."

He drank. "There was more, of course; I touch only the surface. They all began to run together in my mind after a while, and one finds it most difficult to sort out the proper order of events. In one six-month period, never leaving the ship, I sailed under nine different flags."

He drank. "Not being South American myself, and therefore not suspected of patriotic alliances or emotional ties with one side or another, I found that I was considered more trustworthy than most crew members. For that reason I rose rapidly through the ranks to the quarterdeck. In due course I had earned the position and rank of Third Mate, the post I still held when a party of Paraguayans in a stolen skiff rowed out to our ship one dark night and pirated the *San Andreas* from its then-possessors, who may have been Brazilians. Or Costa Ricans, I forget which. Paraguay, which is a landlocked nation as you know, had been at some considerable disadvantage in possessing no navy of its own. Therefore, the capture of the *San Andreas* was a victory of signal importance to that nation. The *San Andreas* became the whole of the Paraguayan Navy. As a matter of fact I suppose she still is."

He drank. "Shortly thereafter, however, Paraguay lost its several wars. As a result our captain and his men were understandably reluctant to venture ashore anywhere on the South American coast, for fear of encountering hostile forces whose brutality was well known to us all. Therefore, we fled northward and, after many peregrinations and misadventures, we finally arrived at the Golden Gate, and found a berth for our weary ship here in San Francisco.

"The captain and his crew at once deserted the ship and set out for the gold fields. I had been promoted Second Mate on the voyage up, and after a suitable interval alone on the ship I appointed myself Acting First Officer. Sometime after that, I assumed—not without some audacity, I'm sure—the temporary title of Captain."

He drank. "And all the while I had in my mind the unhappy state my poor Daddy must be in, attempting to run the apothecary shop without my help."

Gabe said, "You've been here three years you say?"

"Yes. I keep myself alive by fishing off the windward side of the ship. But I appear to owe the city three years' worth of dock fees and, in fact, the harbormaster of late has made ominous statements about impounding the ship."

"Your father must be pretty worried about you by now," Vangie said. "How long have you been away from Baltimore?"

Captain Flagway drank. "Twenty-four years," he said. "But I suppose Daddy has made do with temporary help."

Saying which, he passed out and slipped quietly to the floor.

He awoke in the night, and they were all sitting around watching him. They smiled. Someone gave him a drink and he clutched it gratefully.

Gabe said, "Feeling all right now?"

"Just one more swallow—ump—yes, that'll do quite nicely, I'm sure." He beamed.

"Looks to me like you could use a little money, captain."

"Lord, yes. Why the dock fees alone are a terrible worry in my mind, sir."

"I was thinking more along the lines of a railroad ticket to Baltimore."

A bright blue flame of hope burst up in Captain Flagway. "You don't really think that's possible!"

"It isn't," Vangie said flatly. "But he thinks it is."

The captain frowned. "I don't understand."

"Ignore her," Gabe said. "It's only that what we have in mind is—well, maybe just a bit illegal."

"Oh." The captain considered. "I've never done anything illegal," he said. "In fact, now that I think upon it, I've never done most legal things."

"What we're going to steal is the——"

"Oh, dear! Stealing?"

Gabe smiled in an honest and forthright manner. "Well," he said, "maybe that wasn't exactly the right word, Captain. You couldn't really call it stealing, not the way you'd think of what stealing actually is. What we have in mind to do is take the gold from the United States Mint up on the hill there."

Captain Flagway looked at him doubtfully. "That does *sound* like stealing," he said.

"Well, now, just a minute, Captain," Gabe said. "Let's consider this. If I take money away from you, that leaves you in direct trouble. Broke maybe, possibly hungry, or even with bills to pay."

"Like dock fees," the captain suggested.

"That's a good example right there," Gabe agreed. "So if you take something from a man that that man *needs*, that's stealing. Would you say I was right in that?"

"It does sound right to me," the captain said.

"Well, you can't leave the Government broke and hungry," Gabe said. "It just can't be done. The Government isn't a man. Think about it for just a minute here. What is the Government, anyway?"

Captain Flagway shook his head in honest bewilderment. "I haven't the faintest idea," he said.

"Why, my friend," Gabe said, "the Government is your Government, my Government, Vangie's Government, Ittzy's Government, and Francis's Government—even Roscoe's Government. The Government is nothing more nor less than the combined will of all the citizens in the nation—of the people, by the people, for the people."

"That's a nice phrase," the captain said. He nodded, smiling, pleased with it. "You do have a knack for the phrase," he said.

Gabe frowned, thrown off the track for a second. Francis, leaning forward into the conversation, said, "Captain, where were you in, say, sixty-four?"

The captain stroked his jaw, trying to remember. "Let me see," he said. "Sixty-four. That would have been Brazil, I believe, although I may be mistaken."

Gabe said, "Francis, that's neither here nor there. The point, Captain, is that the Government is the people, and *we're* the people. We're citizens, so we're part of the Government."

The captain nodded, seeing the wisdom in that. Beside him, the girl Vangie was giving Gabe looks of astounded admiration, and now she said, "Why, Gabe, I never knew you thought deep thoughts like that."

"I'm thinking all the time," Gabe told her. Back to the captain again, he said, "Getting back to the Mint for a minute—if we take gold from the Government, it's just exactly the same thing as if we switched our own money from one trouser pocket to another, isn't it?"

The captain frowned. He felt all at sea suddenly, though not in any familiar way. He said, "Is it?"

"Of course, it is," Gabe said.

Still trying to work his way through the logic—pretty much like chewing a twenty-cent steak—the captain nodded and said, "I guess I just never looked at it that way."

"In fact," Gabe went on, "the newspapers are saying exactly the same thing. Have you been reading the papers?"

"No, I—I'm afraid I don't——"

"Well, I'll tell you," Gabe said. "The papers are saying that since this so-called financial panic started it's the policy of our Government to get more cash money into circulation. And that's just what we're out to do, my friend."

Francis joined the conversation again. "Why, Gabe, you're right," he said. He sounded surprised and pleased, as though he hadn't expected to find himself in agreement with his friend, though why that should be the captain had no idea. "I do see what you mean," Francis said. "It's actually patriotic, isn't it? Circulating the money."

The captain found himself nodding along with Francis. It seemed to him he could make out light at the end of the tunnel. "It is, isn't it?" he said. "Patriotic. In a way."

"A darn funny way, if you ask me," Vangie said.

Gabe leaned toward the captain. "Then you're in?"

"Well——" Suddenly the captain had a familiar feeling. It was as though he was being crimped again—without the rough hands and the burlap sack, but just as effectively being whisked away into somebody else's plans. Trying to be cautious, he said, "I don't really know. I mean, what would it involve? I couldn't hit anyone on the head, you know, or anything like that."

"No, no," Gabe said, "you wouldn't have to."

"Not hold a gun," the captain went on, "or stab anybody."

Francis and Vangie both looked a trifle green. Gabe, patting the air in a calming manner, said, "No no, not at all. Definitely not."

"I couldn't strangle anybody with my bare hands," the captain explained earnestly. "Or cut them apart with an ax, or bury them in wet cement, or drown them in the sewer, or——"

Francis and Vangie kept leaning farther and farther away, out of the conversation. Gabe too was looking green by now, and his voice was somewhat loud and shrill when he said, "Nothing like that. I promise you, Captain. You don't have to go on; I understand the kind of thing you're talking about. It won't be anything like that at all."

"Well, that's good," the captain said.

Ittzy said, "We just want your boat."

"That's fine," the captain said. He felt great relief. "Then I wouldn't have to throttle anybody or——"

"Just the boat!" Gabe said, fast and loud. Then he lowered his voice again. "Just the boat. To make our getaway in."

"Very good," the captain said, nodding. Then he stopped nodding and frowned. "But I have no crew."

"We'll take care of that part," Gabe said.

Vangie gave him an odd look, one the captain couldn't quite fathom. "We will?" she asked.

Gabe ignored her. To the captain he said, "The question is, will that boat of yours—I mean, I don't want to say anything against her, but she is sort of——"

"A rotting old tub?" Captain Flagway asked.

"Well, yeah. Now," Gabe said, "I figure a million dollars in gold——"

The captain blinked. "A million dollars?"

"——should weigh in at about two and a half ton. Will the *San Andreas* carry that much weight?"

The captain considered the question, then shook his head. "To be absolutely truthful with you," he said, "I really don't know."

"The thing is," Gabe said, "we wouldn't want it to sink with all that gold on board."

"I can see that," the captain said.

Gabe scowled, frowning toward the middle distance. "If there was only some way to test it," he said. "Get two and a half ton of something else on board ahead of time, and see if she kept on floating."

"That would be very good," the captain said.

"Hmmmmmmm," Gabe said.

Francis said, "Old cock, I might have a small suggestion."

17

Ittzy sat in a chair in the center of a big square that was roped off to keep the people from crowding too close to him.

It was on the afterdeck of the *San Andreas*. People were swarming aboard to stare at him. Ittzy stared right back. He was getting sick and tired of all this. With the money they were going to get out of the Mint he'd never have to put up with this kind of attention again.

They had come down to the waterfront in the morning and met Captain Flagway at the dock. Flagway had the physiognomy of a bassett hound anyhow and this morning his eyes were bloodshot and he walked around very carefully balancing his head on top of his neck as if it were about to fall off. Ittzy had never been drunk enough to get hung over and he didn't want to try, judging by the examples he'd seen in the past fifteen years in San Francisco.

When they had arrived at the ship in the cold morning light Gabe had looked at it again and made a sickly face and remarked, "You know I get the feeling the only thing keeping that tub on top of the water is some sandbar it's sitting on. I mean, for God's sake look at it, it's got barnacles growing on top of the *barnacles*."

Francis had said, "Oh, I don't know, old cock, she doesn't look all that dismal to me."

Vangie had said, "I still don't understand this idea of yours."

"My dear, it's simplicity itself. The problem being how do we get two and a half tons aboard the *San Andreas* to test her, without breaking our dear old backs."

"But how does putting Ittzy in a chair on the deck solve that problem?"

"By inducing two and a half tons of human flesh to walk on board the ship, my dear Vangie."

Captain Flagway was keeping them moving right along behind the rope barrier. At the head of the gangplank Vangie was taking the one-dollar-a-head admission charge. And down on the dock at the foot of the plank, Gabe and Francis were counting heads as the gawkers arrived.

It was a nice sunny morning. If it hadn't been for all the people staring at him, Ittzy would have enjoyed sunning himself in the mild balmy breeze on deck. He glanced past the people toward the signs they had put up—lettered in Francis's fine hand—at the head of the dock, announcing that for one day only Ittzy "Good Luck Charm" Herz could be visited on board. Now the crowd on the ship was steadily growing. The idea was to get fifty people on board all at once. Gabe and Vangie had sat down and worked it out with pencils; they figured forty people would weigh about the same as the gold, and the other ten people would equal the weight of the crew they were going to have to find to man the ship.

Ittzy watched Vangie and Gabe and Francis and the captain and he smiled. He had grown to like his new friends.

Down on the pier Gabe called out, "Sorry folks, that's all for today. We don't want to exhaust Mr. Herz, now do we. Visiting day's over. Sorry about that my friend but better luck next time. . . ." He was putting up the chain across the foot of the plank. Some of them were grumbling but gradually they began to turn away.

So there must be fifty people aboard.

The gawking faces were, at least, friendlier than just an eyeball at a time in a knothole.

Then he noticed somebody was starting to bellow and yell down on the pier. He looked that way again, and it was the people who hadn't been allowed on board. They were raising a ruckus, refusing to take no for an answer.

They were crowding forward toward the gangplank. Ittzy heard Gabe's voice raised in protest, trying to head them off, but it wasn't working; a ruckus was starting and it looked ready to assume the proportions of a general brawl. Slowly Gabe and Francis were giving way under the onslaught, and the brawl worked its way up the gangplank. The ship was about to be overloaded for sure.

And here came Mama.

Ittzy could see her, flanked by Officer McCorkle, thundering along the pier like the transcontinental express.

Ittzy got to his feet. He didn't feel that danger threatened —he never felt that danger threatened—but it did seem as though, between the brawl and Mama, life was going to get uncomfortable pretty soon. And on such a sunny day, too.

Vangie and Captain Flagway had both come closer to him now, and flanked him, one on each side. The customers were fighting one another all over the place, and both Gabe and Francis were completely lost to view.

Mama was almost to the foot of the gangplank, coming along the pier at full speed with Officer McCorkle in her wake and brawlers scooting out of her path as though she were a fire engine.

Ittzy, pointing, said, "That's my Mama."

Vangie clutched his arm. She seemed very nervous. "We'll hide you," she said.

"My, yes," said Captain Flagway. "We'll hide you and stay

with you." He seemed in a big hurry to help Ittzy get away from all this, and Ittzy felt immediate gratitude.

The three of them went through a narrow hatchway and down a steep flight of narrow steps—more ladder than staircase—closing the hatch behind them, shutting out the sunlight and some of the noise of the fighting. There were barrels lying around in the semidarkness, so they righted three of those and sat on them to wait things out.

It was dank and foul down here, below decks. Ittzy was about to say that maybe things weren't so bad up above after all when Vangie put a quick finger across his lips and said, "Ssshh. You don't want your Mama to find you here."

No, he didn't. He was also totally undone by the sensation of Vangie's finger actually touching his lips. He whispered, "Uh," three times, rolled his eyes, gulped and remained silent.

Overhead the brawl thumped and thundered. Voices shouted in rage. Someone fired a shot. Vangie cocked her head and said, "That sounds like Gabe's knuckle-duster. Maybe it'll scare them off."

Ittzy listened to the racket with his eyes tight shut. *Oh please don't let Mama find me down here.* He thought again of all that gold. Freedom.

"Somebody's coming," the captain said softly.

"Shhhhhh," Vangie said.

Footsteps. Up above, the shrilling of police whistles and the stomp of boots on deck.

The bulkhead door opened slowly. Ittzy didn't open his eyes; he buried his face in his hands. If Mama caught him now, here like this, she'd chain him into that peephole room and throw the key away.

"Oh, here you are."

It was Gabe's voice. Ittzy looked up in vast relief.

Francis was with Gabe. They both looked disheveled. Gabe's soft cap was tilted far over on his head, about to fall off. Francis's cape had a rip in it. There was a big bruise on Gabe's cheekbone.

They closed the door behind them and sat down on water-kegs. "Let's just sit tight till the cops clear those damn fools off the decks," Gabe said.

"Oh dear," Francis said, "they've ruined my cape, utterly ruined it."

"You'll have enough to buy a cape *factory* in a few days," Gabe growled. Then he brightened. "Must be eighty, ninety people up there stomping around. At least we know the old tub holds up all right."

The ship was creaking and settling a little, but she did seem to be remaining afloat. Ittzy listened for the unmistakeable sound of Mama's tread, and he was sure he heard it several times. He shivered and made himself smaller in the dark corner.

Gabe was beginning to look oddly weak and pale. He cleared his throat several times and said, "Okay, okay, the boat's all right, now we need a crew. Come on now, everybody think. Any suggestions?"

Ittzy tried to think, but all he could think about was Mama up there on deck. Dust was shaking down from the beams overhead; the pounding continued up there, the police whistles shrilled much nearer, and Ittzy recognized Officer McCorkle's hoarse voice.

Francis said, "Well, you may not agree with this, old cock, but actually there's only one man for that job."

"Who?"

"Roscoe Arafoot."

"Who?"

"You know. The chap who was crimping Captain Flagway yesterday."

Flagway said, "You must be daft. You'd have dealings with that scoundrel?"

"You *do* want a crew, don't you? Well, dears, that's Roscoe's job. Everyone's an expert at something, and crew-getting is Roscoe's specialty. Besides, I'm sure I can—ah, handle him. You needn't worry your gentle hearts."

"But he's a—a blackguard, sir!"

"Yeah," Gabe intervened. "But Francis is right. The guy can recruit guys for a crew for us." He looked up at the dust that was still coming down from the beams in puffs and clouds. "Soon as this weather clears let's go have a talk with the son of a bitch."

Captain Flagway was obviously not greatly pleased, but he didn't have anything else to say, and for a few minutes the group sat in silence, listening to the noise from above. Ittzy felt warm in the midst of this group, sheltered amid their friendships. He said, "You don't think my Mama will find me down here, do you?"

Vangie patted his hand, which turned him to jelly all over again. "Don't worry, Ittzy," she said, "you've got us now."

Ittzy smiled. "Thank you," he said. He had never felt so safe.

18

Gabe looked around at the filth in the alley. "This is kind of a tough neighborhood for you to be hanging around, isn't it?"

"Oh I have friends just *every*where," Francis said with a private little smile, and led him into a blind pig.

It was the seventh saloon they'd hit so far. Francis eeled through the packed crowd of sailors and thugs. The bartender looked up, Francis caught his eye, and Gabe heard the bartender's answer to Francis's question:

"Yeah, he's here. Back there someplace. Watch you don't get trampled to death."

Clatter of glass on glass, scrape of bootsoles and chairs, drone of hard masculine voices, odors of spilled whisky, heavy tobacco smoke and stale beer. The place had a low ceiling and the light was bad. Gabe felt constricted; he wanted out. But he followed Francis, who moved through the crowd with effortless insouciance.

Gabe had seen a lot of dives. This was probably the lowest he'd ever been in.

Maybe there was hope for San Francisco yet.

Francis suddenly lifted on tiptoe, waving a hand over his head and saying, "Oh *there* he is. Yoo-hoo, Roscoe!"

The burly guy at the table in the far corner lifted his head from a schooner of beer, looking a little meaner than a barracuda with a toothache. Approaching, Gabe caught his first whiff and slowed down. He closed the rest of the distance to the table with a reluctance that increased in direct proportion to the smell.

Roscoe wore his customary vicious snarl but when he recognized Francis skipping toward him through the crowded tables he paled and looked around very quickly as if he suddenly wanted to know where the exit was, or as if he wanted to pretend he wasn't there at all.

"Roscoe, we've been looking all *over* for you."

"Yeah, yeah," Roscoe muttered. He buried his face in the glass.

Francis sat down. Gabe hung back and tried to avoid breathing.

"Now, Roscoe dear, do stop pushing your face in that beer a minute. We're not here to threaten you."

Somehow Gabe got the feeling it wasn't the threat of physical violence that was making Roscoe bashful.

Roscoe pushed his chair back. "I got an appointment."

"We must talk with you, Roscoe."

"Yeah. Well. Some other time." Roscoe was on his feet, edging around the table.

Gabe could see it was impossible. Roscoe just couldn't think about business with Francis around. He reached out a detaining hand; before Roscoe could bat him out of the way, he said quickly, "I want to talk a little business—friend."

Roscoe stopped working up his rage long enough to give Gabe a look.

Gabe said, "Francis, don't forget that fire-alarm job you've got to do. Why don't you start on that now; I'll talk to friend Roscoe here."

Francis nodded regretfully. "That might be best, I suppose. But don't go away, Roscoe, I'll be back, dear." He beamed with half-lidded eyes, looked Roscoe up and down, and slipped quickly away.

They watched him go, and then Roscoe sat back down and poked his beetle-browed face into the schooner. "Need another one," he muttered. "You want something, friend?"

"Sure. Beer."

"You buying?"

"Why not," Gabe said expansively.

Roscoe waved at somebody and made hand-motions that conveyed a two-beer message. Then he sat back and glowered. "Well?"

"I need a crew."

"For a ship? You don't look like no ship captain to me. You look like a dude."

"Yeah. Well I expect you and I will get that sorted out sometime. In the meantime I've got a ship and it needs eight or ten guys."

"You want 'em crimped, huh?"

"No."

"Eh?"

"They've got to be willing."

"You want *volunteers?* Friend, you come to the wrong guy."

"Look, it's just a short trip."

"How short?"

"A day. Maybe two."

"What kinda ship?"

"Captain Flagway's boat: the *San Andreas*."

"The *San Andreas?*"

"It's not my fault."

"Sheee, that tub. A lot of guys be scared to set foot on her—you never know when some timber's gonna give out from under your foot."

"This job'll pay pretty high for just a day or two's work."

"How high?"

"What'll the traffic bear, Roscoe?"

Roscoe brooded at him. "Depends, kinda. Where you going?"

"Away from San Francisco. Not far."

"What's the cargo?"

"Just a wagonload of stuff."

"One wagonload and you need a big old tub like that?"

"Well, it'll be kind of heavy."

The beetling brooding stare fixed him suspiciously. "You gonna have bluebottles on your tail, right?"

Gabe hesitated. "Well it's possible, yeah."

It made Roscoe snort. "Sheee. That tub of Flagway's, you couldn't outrun a garbage barge in that. Cops got some nice speedy little police-boats out there in the Bay, you figure on that? How you gonna outrun them?"

"I figured on the fog maybe."

"No good. It don't last long enough."

"We'll wait for a fog."

"Not interested, friend."

"Now that's too bad, Roscoe, I was just about to offer you the opportunity to earn yourself five thousand dollars for two days' work." Gabe started to rise. "Maybe I'll see you sometime."

"Siddown."

"Hmm?"

"Well, I just had an idea, see."

Gabe sat back down. "And?"

"I got a brother name of Captain Percival Arafoot. You ever hear of him, maybe?"

"Can't say as I have."

"Hell, he's the only guy on the Barbary Coast tougher than me."

"Is he now."

"You disputin' that, friend?"

"Not just now, Roscoe. Go on about your brother."

"Well he's got this ship, see. The *Sea Wolf*. Now this here's a *fast* ship, friend."

"Where is it?"

"Right now? Up north someplace. What he does, my brother, he smuggles Alaska seal furs down to Seattle; that's how come he's got a fast ship. The *Sea Wolf's* gotta be able to outrun the Coast Guard, see."

"So?"

"So my brother Percival just might be interested in this little operation of yours."

"Sounds interesting," Gabe said.

"Course him and me, we'd want a piece of your operation. Not just a fee."

"No deal. Five thousand for you, five thousand for him."

Roscoe considered it.

Gabe said, "You think you could get him down here pretty quick?"

"If you make it worth his while. Say ten thousand."

"Six."

"Nine."

"Seven."

"Eight," Roscoe said, "and that's my last offer."

Gabe figured maybe brother Percival would see three thousand of it if he was lucky, which would leave Roscoe with five thousand of Percival's and another five thousand of his own.

Enough to make him happy anyhow.

"Done," Gabe said.

"Okay. I'll send him a telegram. Ought to reach him soon—he's due into Seattle right about now."

"Fine—fine," Gabe said. "But I still want a crew for the *San Andreas.*"

"I thought I just told you——"

"I know what you told me. But two ships are better than one in this operation."

"You gonna tell me what it's all about now?"

"Later," Gabe said. And left.

From the door he looked back and saw Roscoe's eyes glinting at him over the rim of his beer schooner like a pair of gun muzzles.

19

Vangie, through dressing, got up from the bed to yawn and stretch, limbering up her body for the new day. Then, idly scratching her waist at the right side, she turned slowly to limber her mind with a daytime view of the room they'd spent the night in. She liked nice places and this was a nice place, all rose brocade and mahogany finials.

They had to be early risers, she and Gabe, to be ahead of the hotel maid service, but it was still late enough so plenty of morning sunlight poured through the two wide windows, gleaming on the china pitcher and glistening from the tiny prisms dangling from the kerosene lamps.

Finishing her turn Vangie looked over at Gabe, who was standing by one of the windows and admiring the silver snuffbox, turning it around and around in the sunlight. His Eastern feistiness and odd hunched way of standing, once so foreign, were dear to her now. It was hard to remember what life had been without Gabe; harder to try to visualize a future life without him. But if he persisted in this Mint business, and if he kept piling one danger atop the other . . .

Well. She'd decided not to brood about that, and so she

wouldn't. Walking across the room to where he was still fooling with the silver snuffbox, she said, "I was never so surprised in my life as when that went off."

Gabe shook his head, and hefted the snuffbox-gun in his palm. "One of these days," he said, "you're going to stick your hand in somebody's pocket and blow your fingers off. Or his behind."

"Maybe I *ought* to reform," she said. And she was thinking it might be worth it, turning honest, if she could get him to do the same. Keep him from the Mint, keep him from Roscoe Arafoot.

But he said, "You'll be able to afford reform pretty soon."

Hiding her disappointment, she nodded at the snuffbox. "You want it?"

"No, I've got enough." He handed it to her. "Sell it," he said, "we can use the money. It can help us set up for the big job."

"Gabe, I know you don't like me trying to talk you out of that idea, but——"

"That's right. I don't."

"——but I do want to say one thing. Can I just say one thing?"

"Which thing? San Francisco's better than New York, or you can't rob the Mint?"

"Neither."

He gave her a surprised look.

"All I wanted to say was, please don't have anything to do with those Arafoot brothers. They've got the meanest reputations of anybody along the coast, and they've earned them."

"Listen, sister, I can handle any six non-New Yorkers you can name."

"You're underestimating them, Gabe, I promise you. And even if you *do* get that gold, which is impossible to start with, they'll kill us all to take it away from us if they find out we've got it."

"Look don't worry about it, Vangie. I've got everything all worked out."

"You just think you have. You've never met Captain Arafoot."

"I've met Roscoe. That's enough."

"Roscoe's the kind one," Vangie said. "I really wish you'd reconsider this, Gabe."

"Yeah, yeah," he said. But he wasn't listening. He said, "Listen, I wanted to talk to you about something more important."

"More important? More important than trying to save your life?"

"I know, I know." He walked away from the window, nodding, hunch-shouldered, so totally into his own head she knew it was hopeless to try to attract his attention. "I need a wagon," he said.

She didn't realize he meant he wanted a wagon from *her* until he turned and looked at her and said, "Okay?"

"Okay? What's okay?"

"The wagon."

She pointed at herself. "You want *me* to get a wagon?"

"I need it tonight," he said. "At three A.M. Up by the Mint."

"Gabe," she said, "I pick pockets, not livery stables."

"Oh," he said. He seemed a bit surprised, but not very disappointed. Shrugging, he said, "I just figured you could get us anything we needed. You've been providing pretty good so far. Okay, I suppose I can go ask Roscoe."

"Wait!"

He glanced at her, one eyebrow lifted.

A wagon. She thought desperately, then gave one quick nod and said, "All right. I'll do it."

· *141* ·

He smiled, as sunny and cheerful as the day outside. "Good girl," he said.

"A wagon," she said. "Tonight, at three."

He nodded and pointed skyward. "Up by the Mint," he said.

20

From the main gate of the Mint the street ran downhill two or three blocks. Then it humped up over a lower hill before it swept all the way down the steep pitch to the waterfront flats, across them and out onto the *New World* pier. Since the *New World* was en route to or from Sacramento at the moment, the pier was empty.

That little hump—actually it wasn't so little—was what bothered Gabe. Everything was downhill, except that stinking hump.

He stood near the wall of the Mint, gazing down at the hump and past it to the rooftops beyond. Gaslights illuminated the streets and the fog was a thin mist tonight. The chill was in his bones.

Roscoe—whom Gabe had positioned strategically downwind—said, "It's after three. Where the hell is she?"

"She'll be here."

"You can't trust 'em," Roscoe said.

Francis, who stood watching between Captain Flagway and Ittzy, said, "Listen."

"To what? The damn fog?"

"Shut up, Roscoe dear."

Gabe heard the slow clop of hoofs.

"That'll be her," he said.

The buckboard came in sight, pulled by a weary and bony horse. Vangie was driving it.

Gabe grinned at her. "Knew you'd do it."

Roscoe said, "Where'd you pinch the wagon?"

Francis was stepping forward as the wagon stopped, and Vangie wrapped the reins around the brake handle. "It looks familiar to me," Francis said suspiciously.

Gabe looked at it more closely. "Yeah. Me too."

Vangie climbed down. It was Captain Flagway who had presence of mind to step forward, take her elbow and help her down.

She turned and said brightly, "All right. Now you get to tell me what it's for."

"Wait a minute," Gabe growled. "You're changing the subject."

"I am?"

"Vangie."

She was all innocence. "Yes?"

"Where'd you get the wagon, Vangie."

"Why?"

"Because it looks damn familiar, like Francis says. I've seen this wagon before."

"Of course you have. You've ridden on it before."

"Yeah. That's what I thought." Gabe threw his arms up, beseeching the sky for help.

Vangie turned to Francis. "What's the matter with him?"

Francis said, "Vangie."

"Yes Francis?"

"You hired the wagon, didn't you. You rented it."

"Well——"

Gabe said, "Damn it, if I'd wanted to *rent* a wagon I'd've

done it myself! What do you think we needed *you* to get a wagon for?"

"Well, you mean you actually expected me to steal a wagon right off the street?"

"Yeah. Yeah."

"But why?"

"Because there's a chance there won't be any wagon to return to the owner."

Captain Flagway looked alarmed. "Oh my."

Roscoe gave a disgusted grunt. "Look, what's the matter with alla you? You rented the wagon from the livery stable, right?"

"Yes," Vangie said, still very confused.

"You don't figure the wagon's gonna be in one piece after we do this thing tonight, right?"

"Right," Gabe said.

"So what's the problem? We get all done, I go down and have a little talk with the hostler. I tell him the young lady parked the wagon on the street, and some no-good back-stabbin' thief stole it while she wasn't lookin.' What's the problem?"

Gabe pondered it. "That might work all right. But we'll all have to make damn sure nobody sees our faces. A hundred people will probably see exactly what happens to this wagon."

"So it was whoever stole it that wrecked it, that's all," Roscoe said. "Jeez, you guys worry about the weirdest things."

Vangie turned to Gabe. "I still want to know what you're going to do with it."

"You see this hill?"

She turned and looked. Down, up, and down again. "What about it?"

"Well, we need to find out if the wagon can get up enough speed from here to get up over that hump and keep on going."

She shook her head in bafflement. "I don't understand. Don't you think the horse can pull it up over that little hill?"

"We don't want a horse."

"No horse?"

"No horse. If it'll roll past that hump on its own, it'll get up ten times the speed of any horse alive when it starts down the far side. It's the only way to outrun the guys that'll be chasing us."

"You mean you're just going to let the wagon roll by itself?" she said in awe.

"Well, Ittzy's going along to steer and handle the brakes."

"Oh," she said, and nodded slowly as though it all made perfect sense.

Gabe grinned and patted her cheek, and turned away to help the others make ready. They unhitched the horse and turned the wagon around until its tailgate wasn't far from the main gate of the Mint. The guards couldn't see what was happening from their posts, although they might hear an occasional noise. But nobody was trying to break into the Mint, so they probably wouldn't get too curious.

Ittzy got aboard and braced the wagon tongue between his knees to steer. He put one foot up against the brake handle so he could lean on it if he had to. "Okay. I'm ready."

Gabe nodded to Roscoe. The four men got behind the tailboard—and gave a mighty push.

The wagon rolled away. It picked up speed pretty quickly on the slope, and Gabe was grinning when it zipped through the bottom of the U and caromed on up toward the hump.

His grin halved when he saw the wagon slowing.

Ittzy was steering precisely up the middle of the street. It was almost half past three in the morning; there was nobody else anywhere around. But that didn't mean much now because the wagon was faltering, slowing to a speed a crippled snail could have outrun—and stopping, hesitating, pausing a long daguerrotype silent frozen pause, and then rolling back down toward the trough. . . .

Francis looked ready to burst into tears. Gabe felt the same way. Two blocks below them the wagon pendulumed back and forth, rolling halfway up one hill, then halfway up the other, until Ittzy at last set the brake and locked it in position at the bottom of the trough.

"Damn it," Gabe said.

Roscoe said, "I think maybe you need another plan, bub."

Vangie said, "Don't give up so quickly. Good Lord, you *men!*"

Gabe turned an unfriendly eye on her. "Yeah? What's your idea, then?"

"Simple," she said. "You just need more weight on the wagon that's all, to carry it over the top."

Roscoe said, "What the hell difference that gonna make?"

Vangie told him, "Obviously, Roscoe, you just don't understand the basic principles of mass and inertia and momentum."

"The *what?*"

Gabe said, "Well, it's worth a try. Let's lead this nag down there and lug that wagon back up."

Roscoe said, "What do we fill it up with? We gonna go next door, get the borrow of some gold?"

"We'll fill it up with us," Gabe said. "We must have seven hundred pounds among the five of us, let's see what difference it makes."

Roscoe shrugged and said, "I'll try any damn fool thing once. This can't be worse than the mushroom that Mex girl give me that time."

They all walked down the slope together, Roscoe leading the horse. Francis said to him, "What sort of mushroom?"

"Don't ask me. Girl said it would put me in heaven, but

if that was heaven I'm just as glad I'm due for the other place."

They reattached horse to wagon, and all rode back up to the top of the hill again, near the entrance to the Mint. Then, while everybody else stayed aboard, Roscoe got off, unhitched the horse, tied it to a handy lamppost, and went back around by the tailgate. "Everybody ready?" he asked.

"No," everybody said.

Roscoe waited till everyone was set, with a secure grip on some part of the wagon or one another. Then he gave a strong lunging shove on the tailgate, enough to get the wagon trundling slowly forward, and leaped on board with all the others.

Ittzy had a harder time steering with the added weight, but he managed to keep the wagon more or less in the middle of the street. Gabe watched with dubious hopes; they didn't seem to be gathering much speed at all.

But pretty soon the wagon picked up some acceleration, then some more, and all at once they were rushing forward, swooping down the first slope much faster than before.

"Gaaaaabe!" Vangie cried. Looking at her, Gabe saw her expression combined in the strangest way pride with alarm. He grinned at her and faced front again, into the wind.

A real wind; the wind of their passage. The wagon was really tearing downhill now. The wheels racketed down the cobblestones; he thought for a second the whole contraption would fly apart, but in the noise, wind and rush there was nothing to do but hold on.

The horseless wagon thundered ahead. It whammed down through the trough, whizzed up the second slope, whipped over the top without even slowing down, and gathered juggernaut speed down the second hill toward the Bay far far below. . . .

He grabbed Vangie, hugging her to him. Through wind he shouted, "It works!"

She didn't look all that ecstatically happy.

He grabbed Ittzy's shoulder. "Okay," he yelled. "Slow us down now."

Ittzy braced both feet against the brake handle. "It won't— I can't—it's going to——"

Gabe and Roscoe both dived for the brake handle. Gabe almost fell off. Sparks flew from the brake shoes against the iron tires and the brake handle bent, but it didn't do a bit of good. The wagon flew. It kept going faster—and faster—and faster. . . . Straight toward the pier. . . .

He had a glimpse out of the corner of his eye: Officer McCorkle, standing under a streetlight, his eyes wide open and his notebook wide open. He was shaking his head and licking his pencil.

Gabe braced himself. He gathered Vangie to him, cushioned her with his arm and chest. "HANG ON!"

Startled faces along the street watched as they whizzed between the dives and grog shops straight toward the river-boat pier. . . . Vangie was shrieking, but he couldn't make out what she was trying to say until he turned his head and caught her words distinctly:

"Make it stop! Make it stop! *I just did my hair today!*"

The brake handle snapped.

The wagon careened onto the pier, going just a little faster than a greased sled on an icy mountainside. Ittzy steered neatly around a crated cast-iron boiler. Vangie yelled something, Gabe clutched her close, Roscoe lost his footing and went tumbling around in the wagon bed. Captain Flagway started praying in Spanish, and Francis closed his nostrils with thumb and forefinger.

Gabe stared straight ahead, and the nighttime world gradually filled with water. Black, cold, wet water.

"No," Gabe said, very quietly and very privately. The wagon flashed right out to the end of the pier, straight out *past* the end of the pier, wheels spinning against air, shooting out into space as though it had been fired from a brass cannon.

There was an instant's sense of motionlessness, as safe and solid as a hotel room, and Gabe looked around at a view of San Francisco and its Bay that he'd never had before. Then the trajectory of the wagon curved downward, and water was dead ahead, and the buckboard landed in the choppy Bay like a bartender's palm slapping down on a double eagle.

Everybody went rolling and tumbling, joining Roscoe in the wagon bed. Gabe found himself wrapped around Vangie, the two of them pasted to the back of the buckboard seat. And already water was spurting in through gaps between the boards.

Gabe didn't even care. Water an inch deep in the wagon and rising, and he was too happy to even notice the stuff. He struggled to his feet, pulling Vangie with him, and clutched the side of the wagon. Water was pouring in everywhere, and he had a big idiotic smile on his face. He stared uphill toward the Mint far far away and toward the horse standing alone way up there, hitched to the lamp-post and chewing away slowly in mild amaze. "It works," he said, in an awed half whisper.

Vangie gave him a bleary look.

"It works!" Gabe cried. He spread his arms and crowed, shouting, "I *knew* it would work!"

The jumble of people on the water-covered floor around him looked up with several expressions on their faces, none of them as happy as his. The wagon steadily sank, and Gabe stood in it, looking all around at the rising perspective and grinning from ear to ear.

21

Somewhere off Puget Sound the *Sea Wolf* made heavy going through a tart sea. A pilot boat from Seattle came alongside, and a yellow sheet of paper passed from its deck to the hand of a sailor on board the *Sea Wolf*.

Crung, the first mate, stood on the quarterdeck and watched the sailor climb toward the captain's cabin, the door of which was closed as always. Timidly the sailor went along there and knocked, and from within a colossal *Roar* bellowed at him. It made Crung wince—even Crung, who weighed two hundred and thirty pounds and had beat up eight railroad men at once in a saloon brawl.

He watched the sailor hesitantly enter the captain's cabin, shaking with fear. The *Roar* got louder and angrier. Very quickly the sailor, pale and quaking and no longer carrying the telegram, came windmilling out of the cabin again. He slammed the door and leaned his back against it weakly, mopping his brow.

From within, the *Roar* continued for a moment or two before it dwindled to an interested grumble.

Crung relaxed a bit. At least the telegram, whatever it contained, hadn't made Captain Percival Arafoot angry, and that was a blessing. Crung remembered the last time the captain had been angry and, remembering, he shuddered gently all over like a sail in an uncertain breeze.

22

Francis strolled casually around the waterfront district wearing the expression of someone who has lost something and is looking for it without much hope of finding it.

He turned a corner past Mme. Herz's Emporium and strolled on. Around him heaved and surged the business life of a busy ocean port; activity pleasantly masculine, for the most part, if perhaps a bit too overripe taken as a generality. The admixture of Oriental grace notes served as a delicate contrast to the grosser elements of the scene; a cargo of Chinese temple bells, for instance, setting off and in a way commenting on the lusty obscenities of Irish and Scandinavian stevedores loading a grand piano onto a packet intended for a brothel in Nome.

But it wasn't for a study in whimsical mongrelization that Francis had come down to this roaring reeking part of town. He had serious business of his own to transact, if only he could find just the right circumstances.

Hmmm. In an alley between a whore shop and an incense importer's rickety warehouse a little tramp was hunkered over a small fire built of scraps, cooking a fish in a battered piece of tin shaped to the general outlines of a frying pan. Glancing in at the serious hunched back of the man, Francis paused and considered. Would he do? He would do.

Francis entered the alley, nodded amiably at the tramp and said, "Afternoon."

"Yuh," said the tramp. His concentration remained on his fish, but a certain bunching of his shoulder muscles indicated his awareness of—and attitude about—Francis's presence.

"My, that smells good," Francis said and smiled in a way that he hoped was disarming.

Not looking up, and so not disarmed by the smile, the tramp said in a sandpaper voice, "Not enough for two, pal. Sorry."

"No, no," Francis said, refusing the unmade offer with a fluttering of his fingers. "I wouldn't think of it. A man's dinner is a sacred thing."

The tramp nodded. "I always figured it that way," he said, giving his fish a poke with a little bent twig.

"It was as a fellow gourmet I was speaking," Francis told him.

"Yeah?" Noncommittal, still not looking up.

"The aroma," Francis said, "tells me you have the chef's touch."

Now at last the tramp did look up, suspicion and growing wonder conflicted in his expression. He faced Francis's disarming smile and said, "Yeah?" This time, with more credulity in it.

"You don't simply burn your food and shove it into your gullet," Francis assured him. "You *prepare* it." He spread his hands, as though smoothing sheets. "You *respect* it." His fingertips touched, in a semi-religious gesture. "You *care for* it." His hands closed slowly, gently around a ball of air.

The tramp smiled upward in awe. "Yeah," he said. He was amazed at himself. "Yeah, I do."

· 154 ·

Francis sniffed, beamed in rapture, and closed his eyes, expressing ecstacy. He sniffed again, aware of the tramp's open-mouthed observance of his performance. He permitted a tiny purr to escape his closed mouth. He sniffed a third time— and paused. A tiny frown. One eye open. Doubt, hesitation. He appeared to question the lambent air.

The tramp looked worried. He too sniffed, with a noise Francis could have done without. He said, "Something wrong?"

Francis cocked his head to one side like a fox hearing the hunter's horn. He sniffed. "It's——" he said, and paused to consider. His fingers dibbled in the air before his face. Sniff. "It's cooking too—slowly," he decided.

The tramp was barely breathing. He stared at Francis like a child at a magician, a bird at a snake.

Francis nodded, slow and deep. "Yes," he said. "Too slowly." He gave the tramp an open, honest, concerned look, as between equals. "Don't you sense it?"

The tramp turned his head to blink at his fish. "Yeah?"

"It's the breeze through the alley," Francis announced. "You know, if you were to push the fire a bit closer to the wall there . . ."

"Ya think so?"

"It will make all the difference," Francis told him. "Here, I'll help."

Between them, using other scraps of wood, they pushed the tiny fire over closer to the incense warehouse wall. The part Francis moved came right up next to the wall, though the tramp couldn't see that from the other side.

"There," Francis said, rising again and dusting off his knees. "Much better. You should start slicing your onion now."

The tramp frowned. "My onion?"

Francis expressed disbelief. "You're roasting fish without an onion?"

Embarrassed, the tramp moved his hands around vaguely and wouldn't meet Francis's eye. "Well, I, uh——"

"I'll give you mine."

The tramp looked at him, astonished. "Aw, say, pal——"

"No, I insist."

Francis took an onion from his pocket and held it up between thumb and first finger, again like a magician. "I can always get another," he said, and smiled fondly at the onion, as though he and it had been through much together that neither would ever forget.

"Pal," the tramp said, "you're a sport."

"Think nothing of it." Francis cleared a bit of ground away from the fire, and placed the onion in it like a model of the Taj Mahal. "Now," he said, "you slice it here."

"Right." The tramp pulled a folding knife from his pocket, opened it, rubbed it against his filthy pants, and hunkered over the onion. As he sawed carefully away, the pink tip of his tongue showed at the left corner of his mouth.

"Slice it very thin," Francis told him, "and spread it *over* the fish when you turn it for the last time. When the onion edges begin to brown, the fish is done. Just pour your butter sauce over it, and——"

"Yeah, yeah," the tramp said, sawing away. He tried to look like a man with a butter sauce. "That's right, yeah."

Francis gave him a look. "No butter?"

The tramp put down his knife and patted his pockets. "Today I kinda, you know, I was roughing it."

"Well, you go ahead and slice your onion," Francis told him, "and I'll go get the butter."

"Say, pal, you don't have to——"

"Fine cooking is its own reward," Francis said. Smiling again, he left the tramp slicing away at his onion, back to the fire. Already the warehouse wall was getting a charred look to it.

Francis walked back around the corner and past Mme. Herz's; a block later he found Officer McCorkle strolling along amid the heaving and the shouting, studying the world in silent suspicion. Francis hurried to catch up, calling, "Officer! Officer!"

McCorkle turned around, and glowered. "You," he said, without pleasure.

"Excuse me," Francis said, breathing a bit heavily. "I don't know the proper thing to do under the circumstances."

"What circumstances, Calhoun?"

"Is it necessary for me to find a fireman," Francis asked, "or can I report the fire to you?"

"WHAT??"

Francis turned and pointed. A block and a half away smoke was billowing from the mouth of the alley, and so was the tramp.

McCorkle leaped into the air and landed running. He and the tramp passed one another on the fly, the one headed toward the alley and the other away from it. Francis grabbed the tramp's arm as he raced by, and pressed a silver dollar into his plalm. "Eat in restaurants," he suggested. "It's safer."

"You're a champ, pal," the tramp said, and raced on, clutching the dollar.

Francis strolled alleyward. McCorkle came battling his way out to the street again from the smoky alley, waving his arms in front of his face, coughing and wheezing. He stared wildly around, blinking through his tears, and ran to the fire-alarm box on the corner. As he began madly to crank the alarm, Francis took from his pocket the large pocketwatch Gabe had lent him and studied its slowly sweeping minute hand.

Alarm bells, at a distance. Francis nodded, still studying the watch.

The bells grew louder with incredible speed. Around the

corner tore the great fire engine, preceded by its lunging white horses. It squealed to a halt at the alley mouth, firemen pitching off and dragging hoses.

Francis clicked shut his pocketwatch, nodded, and ambled away.

23

Vangie watched people walk by the window and listened to men's talk—Gabe and Ittzy and Francis and that horrid Roscoe.

They were all crowded around a table at the window just inside the Golden Rule. Gabe was saying, "Roscoe. How about the crew?"

Roscoe was still antsy in Francis's presence but he was capable of simple sentences. "All set," he said. "I got six guys to handle the ship. The rest of us can pitch in. I mean, we don't want to have to split with too many guys."

"You split up your five thousand however you want."

"Yeah."

"Now tomorrow the *New World's* due to leave for Sacramento at seven in the morning. She won't be back till tomorrow night sometime. That gives us plenty of time. As soon as she's pulled out, I want you to move Captain Flagway's ship to the *New World's* pier."

"No problem."

Vangie sat shaking her head. It was never going to work.

"Now," Gabe said. "Who knows about explosives?"

They all looked at one another.

"Nobody?" Gabe shook his head. "I'm in the middle of mining country," he said, "and I'm at a table with four people, and not one of them knows anything about explosives. You know what the odds are against that?"

Nobody seemed to know that either.

Vangie began to feel a little better.

Then Gabe dashed it. "Well we can't bring in any more new guys at this stage. Ittzy, you're it."

Vangie jerked her head around to stare at him. "What?"

"Sure. Ittzy's our demolition man—we know he's safe. He'll handle the dynamite and he won't get hurt, right?"

Roscoe said, "The what?"

"Dynamite. Some guy invented it over in Sweden. It's a stick explosive. A lot safer to handle than nitroglycerine and a lot bigger bang than blasting powder." Gabe turned to Vangie. "We'll have to get Ittzy a book. You get a book for him, okay?"

"A book?"

"On dynamite."

"A book on dynamite? You want it at the Mint at three o'clock in the morning?"

"Right," Gabe said, grinning, and turned to Francis. "Now about the timing."

"It's all set, old cock."

"Think you ought to double-check it just once more?"

"I suppose it couldn't hurt."

"Well everything depends on that, you know."

"Rest assured, old cock."

Francis went, and Roscoe became much calmer. He said, "You want the ship moved tomorrow, you must be ready to go."

"I am, if your brother's got time to be here by then."

"He'll be here. I been in touch with him."

Vangie brooded unhappily at both of them. She didn't want Gabe to be ready to go, and she especially didn't want anybody having anything to do with Roscoe's brother Percival Arafoot, about whom folks said there was moss growing down his north side.

Gabe said, "The Mint's about to start stamping out coins in the next week or two. That means they're loaded with raw gold now—ingots. That's what we want. There must be upwards of a million in that vault right now."

"A million," Roscoe said, and his face changed.

Vangie closed her eyes. She felt more frightened than she'd ever been. During the preparations the reality of it had receded, but now it was staring her smack in the face. "Gabe, you're going to spend the rest of your life in prison."

"Aagh."

"You've seen the guards. The locks. Everything. You know it can't be done."

"My plan's guaranteed."

"But you saw how many guards they've got, you saw the guns, you saw——"

"I saw the future," Gabe said, "and in it I am very rich."

Sudden sirens started up: fire engine bells. They tore by the window.

Ittzy said mildly, "Seems like a lot of fires lately."

Vangie said dismally, "Then you're definitely going through with it."

"Yeah. And I'll need some things."

She sighed. "Another wagon?"

"No, as a matter of fact. The Mint's got its own wagons, and they're built for the weight. We'll use one of theirs."

"Then what do we need?"

"I'm glad you said we."

She shook her head.

Gabe said, "We'll want the book for Ittzy."

"Check."

"And laughing gas."

"Laughing gas," she said.

"Like the dentists use. Two canisters. And half a dozen sticks of dynamite."

"Dynamite," she said.

"Half a dozen sticks. And a balloon."

"A ba——"

24

The morning of the Great Mint Robbery the fog rolled in very thick and white across the Bay, covering the world as though with the ghost of a great snow. Voices were muffled on the streets, but footsteps sounded with unnatural clarity. Crimpers crimped policemen, prostitutes propositioned one another, and down on Division Street a pickpocket sprained two fingers when he tried to boost a wooden Indian.

Captain Flagway leaned on the taffrail of the *San Andreas*, a pipe in his mouth and a fishing rod in his hands. The line extended down toward the water from the end of the rod, disappearing into the fog at just about the level of the captain's boots; he had to take it on faith that the other end was actually in the water, occupying itself with the business of getting him breakfast.

It was all well and good to be involved in a major robbery scheme, where big numbers like 'one million dollars' were tossed around like apples, but in the meantime life went on. Reality was reality, and a man had to arrange for his own breakfast.

Would the robbery ever actually take place? Would the

captain ever see Baltimore again, his Daddy, and his Daddy's drugstore? Would the harbor master seize the *San Andreas* and thus rob Captain Flagway of the very roof over his head? He stood at the rail, musing on these questions, puffing from time to time on his pipe and occasionally jiggling a bit at the fishing rod, while the fog rolled like great imaginary pillows and his stomach growled gently about the lack of breakfast.

He didn't know he'd been boarded until he heard the clump of boots right behind him. He turned, startled, and out of the fog stamped Roscoe Arafoot and half a dozen toughs who looked like fugitives from Yuma Penitentiary. "Oh!" Captain Flagway said—a tiny cry lost in the fog— and dropped his pole in the drink.

Roscoe said, "We're supposed to move the ship now."

"Oh," Captain Flagway said. He'd thought they were here to crimp him. "Yes," he said, and swallowed. "Well, I'll just——" He pointed in several directions, cleared his throat, twitched and smiled aimlessly, scampering out of their way.

He felt a bit safer in his cabin, with the door more or less locked. That is, the door did have a lock, but a five-year-old child could have gotten through it by leaning on it. Once, off the coast of Peru, a high wind had blown that door open while it was locked. Still, it was the thought that counted, and it relieved the captain's mind somewhat to be able to throw that useless bolt.

Next to the brave door was a porthole, with an all-too-clear view of the deck. The captain stood peeking out this porthole and watched obscure figures moving out there in the fog. At least none of them were moving in his direction.

The fog began to lift as the sails were raised, and soon the full glory of the *San Andreas* could be seen in the thin translucent light of a pale morning sun. The ship's sails looked like patchwork quilts. She tended to heel over at a steep angle on even absolutely calm water, and the bow preferred to dig itself through the water rather than sail over it.

The lifting of the fog didn't do much to lift the captain's spirits. It only meant he could see those ruffians more clearly, and nothing about them reassured him. They looked to be a breed of man which spent much of its time biting other people and being bitten in return. There was a frayed, toughened, gnawed, tooth-marked look about them, with here and there an eyepatch, or a dangling sleeve, or a suspiciously stiff leg.

Slowly the *San Andreas* slipped away from her pier, with Captain Flagway watching through his cabin porthole. The crew might be truculent and frightening, but they appeared competent, moving about their duties in a seamanlike fashion that Captain Flagway himself had never been able to duplicate.

The ship sagged across the Bay toward the pier normally occupied by the *New World*, where the other day they had all gone into the water in the rented wagon. Roscoe's crew tied up broadside to the end of the pier and then ran a pair of wide planks out onto the pier from amidships.

Captain Flagway remained where he was, watching. He'd been present for all the planning discussions, of course, and so knew exactly what was going on, and yet he found himself as fascinated as if all this activity were as mysterious and opaque as the fog had been. People at work. Captain Flagway could watch them forever.

Roscoe went ashore. The crew remained aboard ship, strolling around the deck in a kind of angry, dangerous boredom, growling at one another from time to time like lions irritated by fleas.

The captain stayed in his cabin. His stomach rumbled softly, not like a lion at all.

25

The balloon came sailing through the foggy air. There was utter silence up here, the streets and roofs seen patchily below through breaks in the fog like a dream incompletely remembered. In the basket swaying beneath the great bulb of the balloon sat Gabe, Vangie, Roscoe and Ittzy, each one silent, pensive, waiting, thinking his own thoughts. This was the highest from the ground that any of them had ever been, and none of them much liked it.

Gabe sat on a coil of heavy rope, Roscoe hunkered between the canisters of laughing gas, Vangie stood braced against the side of the basket with her arms folded and her chin lifted in the heroic pose of a woman going down on the ship with her man, and Ittzy sat on a wooden box marked DYNA-MITE and read slowly but soberly in a book titled *THE HANDLING OF A. NOBEL'S DYNAMITE IN CON-STRUCTION, DEMOLITION AND MINING EMPLOY-MENT, Or, The Art Of Explosives In The Modern Age.*

Vangie spoke only once during the voyage through the air. "Gabe," she said, "I want you to remember what I'm saying, in the years to come. You aren't going to get away with this. I'll be baking a fresh cake for you every month in prison—fifty years, that's six hundred cakes."

"Uh huh," Gabe said.

Vangie frowned at him. Then a breeze touched the basket, making it hop, and distracted her into grabbing the suspension cords to keep her balance. By the time she looked back at Gabe, he had twisted around and was watching over the side of the basket toward the ground, looking for landmarks.

It was hard to make things out in the fog. Still, through the occasional wispy holes it was possible to recognize the ornate elaborate decorations on the rooftops of the Nob Hill mansions. One more hilltop to cross, if Gabe's calculations were correct, and they would be over the Mint.

He faced the inside of the basket again. Vangie continued to frown in his direction but had nothing more to say. Roscoe looked almost as uncomfortable in the air as he usually did around Francis. Ittzy continued to read his book, occasionally licking a fingertip and turning a page, then licking the fingertip again and turning the page back, to frown at what he'd already read. The book appeared to be heavy going for Ittzy, but Gabe's confidence in him was undimmed. Ittzy would be all right.

Gabe licked his own finger, and held it up to test the moist foggy wind. It was still on course, easy and steady, leading them to the Mint. He smiled contentedly, ignored Vangie's disapproving looks, and when he next twisted around to look over the side of the basket there was the Mint, dead ahead.

The fog was beginning to break up; they weren't getting here a minute too soon. In ever-largening misty holes in the fog layer Gabe could see the Mint yard down below, with the tour guide gathering his charges for another pass through the interior of the building. It was midmorning now, visiting hours; the main gates were open and people were wandering in, well-surveyed by the guards.

The balloon—brightly colored, painted in astrological and other cabalistic signs, and bearing in great red letters the name PROFESSOR NEBULA (whoever he might be)—drifted over the courtyard and then over the main building of the Mint. At the right point, as he judged it, Gabe yanked the bag-release cord to open the valve and let enough gas out to lower the balloon to the roof.

Nothing happened.

Gabe frowned at the cord in his hand, frowned up at the balloon, frowned over the side at the roof of the Mint, drifting slowly by no more than ten feet below. He tugged again at the cord, and again nothing happened.

Vangie said, "What's the matter?"

"Nothing," Gabe muttered, and yanked at the cord some more. "Not a damn thing."

Everybody was now looking at him in alarm. They were drifting along, at the wind's pace. Soon they'd drift past the Mint and right on out over the Bay. . . . Finally in desperation, Gabe pulled the whisky flask from his hip pocket and shot a hole in the balloon.

Something began to hiss.

But they weren't descending.

Gabe yanked the cord again, but it broke and he stood staring at the useless frayed end in his hand.

They were almost past the Mint when Roscoe removed an enormous horse pistol from his sash and shot a bloody great hole in the balloon.

Now it descended. In fact it descended very rapidly, till the basket thumped solidly onto the roof of the Mint. Gabe was half-crushed by warm bodies; he pushed them away, but the deflating bag of the balloon settled on down and draped itself in billowing folds over them all.

Finally they came batting and pawing their way out from under. Vangie was muttering how she'd known it was never going to work. Ittzy was still reading the book on explosives.

Roscoe emerged with vast pistols in both hands, ready to demolish any army that might appear.

But none did. Evidently nobody had been alarmed by the gunshots. For one thing gunshots were not unheard of in San Francisco. For another it was not an instinctive reaction for people on the ground to look straight up in the air when they heard shots.

When they were sure no one was coming to investigate their arrival on the roof, they all ducked back under the collapsed balloon again to drag out their equipment. Pulling the canisters and the rope and the dynamite, they emerged from the balloon once more and Vangie took the opportunity to whisper in Gabe's ear, "Gabe, this is an omen. Things are going to go wrong. We can still give it up, mix with the regular people in the tour, get out of here just as though it hadnever happened."

He gave her a surprised look. "Everything's fine," he said. "What's the problem?"

Roscoe asked, "What was that thing you were shooting?"

"My flask," Gabe said. "It holds six shots. Vangie picked it up."

Roscoe shook his head in admiration. "They make guns to look like almost anything, don't they?"

"I guess so."

To one side Ittzy continued to read his book.

"Bring the rope," Gabe told Roscoe, and headed for the chimney of the ventilator shaft protruding from the center of the red tile roof. Gabe worked the lid off the chimney, looked around, and said, "Put the book down, Ittzy. Time to go to work."

"This is real interesting," Ittzy said. He seemed pleased and somewhat surprised to find that a book could be interesting. Tucking it away, he came forward to stand patiently while Gabe tied the rope securely around his waist. Then he climbed up onto the chimney and prepared to be lowered down the shaft. His legs went in, his torso went in, and then he stopped.

Gabe said, "What's the matter?"

"I'm too big. I don't fit."

"It's that book," Gabe said. "Give it to me."

Ittzy struggled the book out of his shirt and handed it over, then squirmed around some more. "I'm still too big," he said.

Roscoe said, "It's the gun."

Ittzy had been given one of Roscoe's huge pistols, a weapon chosen more for its impressive appearance than for Ittzy's ability to use it. He said, "But I need the gun. I can't go down without it."

"We'll lower it to you," Gabe said. "Come on, hand it over."

Ittzy hunkered and squirmed upward out of the chimney, got the pistol out of his trouser pocket, handed it over to Roscoe, and tried again.

"Nope."

Gabe looked at him. "What do you mean, nope?"

"I'm just too big," Ittzy said.

"Maybe it's his belt buckle," Roscoe said.

Ittzy told him, "Roscoe, you'll have me naked, first thing you know, but I still won't fit in this godalmighty ventilator shaft. I'm just too *big*."

"Maybe we could sort of press down on you," Roscoe suggested.

"Well, no," Ittzy said. "I don't think you could do that."

"Drat," Gabe said.

Ittzy said, "Can I get out of here now?"

"Yeah, come on out," Gabe said, and stood glaring at the chimney.

"There, now," Vangie said. "It's all over, we can forget it, we can go home."

Gabe turned to look at her. His eyes squinted a bit as he studied her. "Hmm," he said.

She leaned away, watching him suspiciously. "What do you mean, hmmmm?"

"You're smaller than Ittzy," he said.

"Gabe——"

"You'd fit."

"Now, wait a minute," she said. "It's bad enough I'm along here. I'm not going to——"

"It's safe as houses," Gabe told her. "Roscoe and me, we'll just let you down slow and easy."

"I don't want to be let down at all."

"There's nothing to it," Gabe insisted. "And when you get to the bottom, you just do what Ittzy was going to do."

"I'm not Ittzy!"

"I know. You're smaller. Come on," he said confidentially, encouragingly. "You can do it."

She was weakening. "I don't know," she said.

Gabe handed her the pistol Ittzy had been carrying. "Just aim it," he said. "That's all you've got to do."

"I can't." She held it in both hands, struggling. "It's too heavy to point."

Gabe took the pistol away again, reached into his pockets, and handed her the whisky flask and the knuckle-duster. "These'll do, then."

"This is crazy."

He took her aside and peered into her eyes. "Vangie."

"Yes?"

"Do you love me?"

"I——"

"Do you trust me?"

"Well——"

"Okay, then everything's all right. You got nothing to worry about; we'll be right there as soon as you let us in."

"I trust you," she said doubtfully, allowing him to tie the rope around her waist as he had done with Ittzy.

Vangie couldn't climb on top of the chimney, so Gabe lifted her up and lowered her into the top of the shaft like a wine cork. "You're doing fine," he said.

"I haven't gone anywhere yet," she said. Her voice trembled slightly and she had two round patches of white on her cheekbones.

"You're going now," he told her, and Roscoe began paying out the rope.

She saw Gabe smiling and waving by-by, and then there was nothing to see but the filthy dark brick wall of the ventilator shaft. She was lowered in fits and tugs, the rope around her chest under her arms and just above her breasts, causing her to hang hunched up like a vampire bat. "I'm giving up my looks for that man," she muttered in the shaft. "I'm losing my posture for him."

Finally she reached bottom, and could take the confining rope off. She tugged on it to show she had safely arrived, and the rope was whisked back up again. A little blue light showed up there. She gazed upward wistfully, then looked around at where she was instead, which was standing on the grille-framework in the ceiling of the vault-room. She put her face close to the grating and looked into the room.

There wasn't anybody inside. The barred door to the anteroom was locked. Beyond it, through the bars, she could see the backs and shoulders of the two guards who stood facing the other way.

She looked up. Gabe was lowering the canisters on the rope. She caught them, untied the rope, placed them to one side, and waited while they hauled the rope up and lowered the box of dynamite. After it came down, she took out Ittzy's screwdriver and began to unscrew the grating. *This is ridiculous. It'll never work. Not in a million years.*

They hauled up the rope and walked softly across the roof to the back corner. Roscoe tied the rope to a bolt in the corner and they dropped the length of rope down the back wall. Then they slid down to the paved yard one at a time; Ittzy first, then Roscoe, then Gabe. At the bottom Gabe looked at his red palms. "Next time," he muttered, "gloves."

They walked around the building and at the loading platform separated. Gabe and Ittzy walked innocently to the corner of the building and engaged the attention of the guards; behind them, Roscoe shifted one of the empty Mint wagons into position at the end of the handcart rails on the loading platform. Nobody took any notice; he might have been a Mint employee. When Roscoe finished he joined Gabe and Ittzy at the corner and they walked around into the courtyard to join the guided tour.

"Now and then we stamp an issue of five-dollar half eagles, but it don't happen very often here so if you find a half eagle with our stamp on it maybe you want to hang onto it. They're as rare as a pair of clean socks around a bunkhouse."

Vangie had the metal grating unscrewed. She lifted it out of its frame and set it aside on the ceiling beams. She waited until the minute hand of the watch she'd stolen last week came around to exactly ten-thirty, and then she dropped silently into the vault room.

She slipped across the room, keeping close to the wall. At the front corner she turned, went across to the barred door, and waited just inside it.

The tourists entered the anteroom beyond.

". . . rest assured your money's safe. Nobody's ever tried to rob the United States Mint, of course—nobody's ever been stupid enough to try. I reckon someday somebody will, but you probably won't even read about it in the papers because whatever they do they ain't gonna get anywheres near your Gov'ment's gold."

Finally the group turned and left the anteroom. When the tourists turned left, Gabe, Roscoe and Ittzy turned right and waited just around the corner until the group was gone.

Vangie stepped to the barred door. She had the flask in one hand and the knuckle-duster in the other.

"Stick 'em up."

The guards whipped around in amazement and stared at her. "Huh?"

"Stick 'em up. These are guns."

They grinned. One of them pointed to the whisky flask. "That one must have quite a kick," he said.

"I mean it. They really are guns."

"Sure they are." The guard lifted his key ring. "I don't know how you got in there, honey, but you're about to come out." He began to unlock the door.

"Don't make me shoot. Don't make me prove it!" Her voice was rising toward a hysterical pitch.

The two guards yanked the barred door open.

That was when Gabe and Roscoe arrived. Gabe said mildly, "Okay, hold it right there." Ittzy came in behind them. All three were holding guns that actually looked like guns.

Vangie, her voice still shaky, said, "I thought you said you'd be right down."

"We got here as fast as we could," Gabe said.

The guards were getting over their surprise. One of them said, "You'll never get away with this."

Vangie said, "That's what I keep telling them."

"Let's move it along," Gabe said. "We're in kind of a hurry."

Roscoe relieved the guards of their weapons and tied them

up in a corner of the anteroom while Gabe locked the outer entrance—the steel-plated door that fitted right over the incoming handcart rails. Now they were sealed off from the rest of the Mint.

Ittzy and Gabe climbed into the hole in the ceiling; Roscoe stood guard with his huge pistols. Presently the canisters and the box of dynamite made their way down to the floor, whereupon Roscoe carried the gas canisters out into the anteroom and placed one on each side of the door. Ittzy opened the box of dynamite, removed several sticks, got out his book again, and went thumbing through the pages.

Roscoe returned from the anteroom, wheeling the handcart in. "Okay to turn those valves now?"

Gabe said, "Not yet. Come on."

As Ittzy approached the vault, lip-reading slowly in his dynamite book, Gabe led Vangie out to the anteroom, followed by Roscoe. "We'll wait out here," Gabe said. "Ittzy will set the charges in there and then come out here before they go off."

"I don't know," Vangie said, "how I ever got invol——"

There was a sudden explosion.

The three of them turned, open-mouthed, and stared at the doorway to the vault room. A cloud of smoke puffed out through the doorway, and Ittzy came walking out through it, leafing through the book. He seemed mildly bewildered but otherwise unhurt. "I don't know," he said, shaking his head. "It shouldn't have done that."

Awed, Vangie said, "Ittzy, are you okay?"

He looked up from the book, blushed when he met Vangie's eye, and said, "Fine. Uh, I'm fine. Why not?"

Roscoe said, "What about the vault?"

"Right," said Gabe. He and Roscoe hurried into the next room through the settling smoke, with Ittzy and Vangie right behind them. Inside they found the steel door of the vault sagging wide open like a tin can that had been pried apart with a chisel.

And just inside it were piles and piles of dull yellow metal.

"That's the stuff," Gabe said. "I'd know it anywhere."

Roscoe said, "That's pretty."

"The handcart," Gabe told him.

"Right."

Roscoe wheeled the handcart as close as possible to the ruined door and he, Gabe and Ittzy went to work filling it with the ingots, stacking them with loving care.

Gabe said, "Vangie? Get the valves, will you?"

"Right."

Vangie went back to the anteroom and across to the outer door, took a deep breath, held it, opened wide the valves of both canisters of laughing gas, left them hissing, hurried back to the inner room, slammed the steel door shut behind her, and let out the breath she'd been holding.

Ittzy said, "This stuff's *heavy*."

"Keep loading," Gabe told him.

Throughout the building armed men were beginning to react to the sound of the explosion. For most of them, the first reaction was to say, "What was that?" And stand looking blankly at one another. But a few had already remembered the gold and were starting to move, and the rest would catch on any second now.

Down on the waterfront, Francis was ambling along, easy and casual, taking the air. Pausing at an intersection, he glanced uphill toward the Mint, indistinct in the fog. He looked at his watch and moved on along the street until he came to a fire-alarm box. He posted himself near it and waited, the snap-lid watch in his hand.

Vangie tried to lift an ingot, but it was too heavy for her. She stepped back and let the men do it. Her face was filled with anxiety.

Guards ran from all directions through the mazed corridors toward the vault.

The first arrivals found the anteroom door locked. Seven men dashed off in seven directions to find a key.

Vangie was hopping up and down with nervousness. "That's enough," she cried. "That's enough. You've got *enough!*"

"All of it," Gabe said grimly, and dropped another ingot onto the pile in the handcart.

Three guards with three keys crashed into each other at a corridor junction. One was dazed, but the other two rushed into the railway-tracked corridor. After a minor skirmish they got the anteroom door unlocked.

Two men clawed the edge of the door and swung it ponderously open. Twenty-two guards poured into the room and all but trampled one another in their flying rush for the vault.

They didn't have time to notice the two canisters hissing quietly to themselves in a room already filled with laughing gas. Their attention was fixed on that closed steel door to the vault room across the way; midway to it, the guards began to sag. Grinning feebly, they sank to the floor.

Two of them, realizing too late what was going on, tried to get to the canisters to turn them off but failed. Chuckling stupidly, they embraced the cool smooth canisters in flaccid grips, sliding slowly down to the floor.

Three others, at the rear of the group, turned around and made it back to the hallway before collapsing like their mates with idiotic smiles and glazed eyes.

The canisters hissed on, above the supine smiling guards.

Francis took out the watch, glanced at it, and looked upward at the Mint. The fog was thinning more and more with every passing second.

The handcart was full.
Too full.
"Oh no," Gabe said.
Five thousand pounds of gold was a lot of gold. It was in fact too much gold to push.
The four of them leaned as hard as they could, but the handcart wouldn't even rock. It might have been a stone wall.
Damn!" Gabe said. "Damn, damn, damn, damn!"
Vangie cried, "I knew it wouldn't work! I knew it couldn't be done!"
Ittzy said, "I guess we'll have to take a lot of the gold out."
"Over my dead——" And then Gabe whipped around and grabbed Ittzy's arm. "Wait a minute. Wait a minute. Gimme that book!"
Ittzy gave him the book and Gabe thumbed feverishly through it. "I know I saw it in here someplace, someplace . . . Something about *shaped charges*. . . ."

Nervously, Francis paced back and forth, eyeing the fire-alarm box and the Mint up at the top of the hill.

Captain Flagway had remembered a bottle tucked away in his desk, and made it stand for both breakfast and lunch. There was enough left for dinner, plus snacks. Now, he peeked out the porthole and watched Roscoe's crew stacking bales of hay along one side of the ship, at the foot of the mainmast on deck. He reeled back to his chair and took another swallow from the bottle.

Sixteen additional guards piled into the anteroom, collapsing before they reached the second door.

"*I've got it!*" Gabe cried.

"We'll all be getting it," Roscoe said. Discouragement was becoming general.

"Ittzy," Gabe said, "get the rest of the dynamite. All of it. Bring it over here."

So while Gabe held the book open under Ittzy's nose, one finger tracing the words, Ittzy read with one eye and packed all the dynamite into a charge that he fixed to the face of the mangled vault door right behind the immobile handcart.

Ittzy finished and stepped back. "Now what?"

Gabe scowled toward the iron door. "Listen, what if there's guards lying across the tracks out there?"

Roscoe said, "So we run over them."

"No!" Vangie cried.

"Vangie's right," Gabe said. "We don't want them after us for murder."

Vangie said, "I'll go," and before anyone could react she was over by the steel door.

Gabe rushed to catch her. "Wait a minute—*wait* a minute!"

"What for?" She pushed the steel door open an inch. Gabe peered over the top of her head and saw that three of the guards were indeed sleeping across the tracks, broad smiles on their faces.

Vangie pulled the door open just wide enough to slip through. Gabe crowded through behind her, and the two of them, holding their breaths, dashed into the anteroom, dragged the sleepers to one side, dashed back, slammed the door, and breathed.

Roscoe said sourly, "You ready now?"

Gabe smiled at him. "Sure—sure," he said lazily.

"Then let's go."

Gabe smiled. Then he frowned and shook his head to clear it. "I must've got a whiff of that stuff." He glanced at Vangie. "You okay?"

She gave him a sleepy grin. "Hi, lover."

"No, Vangie. Definitely not." He grabbed her arm. "Come on, snap out of it."

"You bet." She kept on grinning and swayed happily toward him.

He put his lips close to her ear. "Think about how we're gonna get caught."

The smile faltered.

"Think about how we'll never get away with it, not in a million years; you warned us and we wouldn't listen to you."

She was frowning again, irritable again. "That's right!"

"That's better." Gabe turned back to Ittzy. "You all set?"

"I suppose so."

"Then let her rip." Gabe crossed to the steel door with two long strides. "Everybody take a few deep inhales and then hold your breath."

There was a lot of huffing and puffing in the room for the next few seconds. Long sighs and heaves of breath. Finally Gabe nodded his head and flung the steel door wide open. A cloud of gas rolled into the vault room. . . .

Ittzy lit the dynamite and they all headed for the corners, holding their breath. Almost instantly the new charge went off.

The blast filled the room with deafening noise and vibration. And emptied it of the handcart, which shot like a cannonball out of the inner room and across the anteroom and right on down the corridor. . . .

And Gabe, Vangie, Roscoe and Ittzy were running like mad, chasing it through the laughing gas and down the long corridor. . . .

· 181 ·

They bolted out of the gas cloud and the pent-up breath exploded from their chests. They ran full-tilt, panting and straining, but the cart was *way* out ahead and it really wasn't any contest.

The cart won.

It shot right off the lip of the loading platform and crashed into the back of the waiting wagon. The blow shook the wagon loose in its tracks and started it rolling toward the main gate with the handcart's dumpbucket tilting over and cascading lumps of gold onto the driver's seat and into the footwell. Two or three ingots fell off and lay in the courtyard, glistening in the mist. . . .

Gabe, Vangie, Roscoe, and Ittzy were still running to catch the damned thing, jumping down off the loading platform and bolting forward at a dead run, toes straining, chests heaving, arms windmilling. . . .

The main gates stood wide open. The two guards there were momentarily paralyzed with disbelief. But now doors in the building began to crash open, and guards came pouring into the courtyard. Roscoe brandished his huge revolvers and fired three quick shots into the air. It made the guards hesitate, just that extra second long enough.

Francis, the watch in his hand for the fifth nervous time, looked up in relief and delight at the sound of the shots. Turning, slipping the watch back into his pocket, he took two quick strides to the waiting fire-alarm box, yanked the handle, and took off at a fast clip for the pier.

Up at the Mint the wagon was closing toward the gate. The ground was level here, so the wagon was gradually losing speed, trundling inexorably but not rapidly toward freedom.

Gabe, Ittzy, Roscoe and Vangie were in its wake, strung out in a ragged line, gasping, running, staggering, slowly overtaking the monster they themselves had created. Guards were rushing at them from everywhere, while other guards scrambled frantically to get the main gates closed in time.

Gabe caught the wagon. He clung frantically to the tailgate, his toes dragging in the dirt as he gasped for breath before pulling himself aboard.

Behind him Roscoe had picked up a trailing Vangie and was holding her under his arm as he barreled forward, looking very nearly as powerful and inexorable as the wagon itself. Trailing the pack came Ittzy, still clutching the dynamite book in one of his pumping hands.

Gabe, lying atop the jumbled ingots, reached back and down to the running Roscoe, who half-lifted and half-threw a squealing, kicking, red-faced Vangie over the tailgate and into his arms. Gabe and Vangie went rolling into the gold, and Roscoe lunged for the tailgate himself.

The guards were running, they were shooting into the air, one or two were even shooting at the wagon. Tourists were scampering in all directions. More guards were pushing against the massive slow-moving gates.

Ittzy scrambled over the tailgate, over Roscoe, over Gabe and Vangie, over the ingots, and finally reached the seat, where he grabbed the wagon-tongue as though it were a tiller, which it was. He didn't even bother to look at the brake, because with all this weight nothing short of total collision was going to stop this juggernaut.

It was roaring right into the gateway. The gates were closing, but not in time. Guards were running, shouting, shooting. Guns were going off and voices were bellowing orders and obscenities. The people on the wagon clung to fragile purchases with toes and fingernails and kept their heads down against the hail of bullets—all except Ittzy, who sat up in plain view and steered and ignored the occasional bullet that skinned a bit of nap from his hat.

Out of the firehouse roared the great fire engine behind its magnificent white horses.

The wagon full of gold and Gabe and Vangie and Roscoe and Ittzy gathered speed as it moved through the gates. A guard lunged for the side of the wagon and clung to it, his feet dragging, until Vangie removed her shoe and rapped his knuckles with the heel, whereupon the guard yelped and let go, and the wagon was through and rolling. . . .

It tipped into the steep downslope beyond the paved apron of the gate area. Now it picked up speed ponderously, clattering and thundering like a battalion of artillery on the march. A block ahead of it, midway down the slope, the great fire engine roared into view preceded by the clangor of its bells.

The fire engine made the turn on two wheels, horses lunging, men straining forward. One or two of them glanced back and saw the gold wagon bearing down on them. Their faces went wide with amazement.

And on ahead of the fire engine the warning bells and sirens were being obeyed. The street emptied of pedestrians and wagon traffic all the way down to the waterfront.

As the fire engine topped the hump of the second hill, the gold wagon roared through the trough and swung up the other side. The wagon slowed perceptibly on the upslope, but Gabe was grinning because he could feel in the seat of his pants that it was going to make it.

And it did. It trundled up over the hump, seeming to hesitate for just a second. During that second the riders had a brief panorama of San Francisco spread out below them. The empty street stretched straight down through it all to the tiny listing absurdity of the *San Andreas* far away at the pier.

Gabe glanced to one side because a flash of red caught his eye. It was the red hair of Officer McCorkle, watching without expression. When the wagon began to gather speed on the downslope, McCorkle took his big notebook out, licked his pencil, and began to jot something in his laborious hand.

Now there was no time for anything but hanging on desperately while the fire engine preceded the wagon straight toward the docks, clearing the way, clanging and whooping, with the wagon catching up on it from behind.

"We're gaining too fast!" Gabe yelled at Ittzy. "Hit your brakes!"

"They won't work!"

The wagon was still accelerating, and the red rear end of the fire engine was getting closer and closer. . . . A pool table wouldn't fit between the two vehicles now. . . . A horse could jump between them now. . . . A man couldn't squeeze between them now. . . .

Gabe opened his mouth to yell, and the fire engine squealed around a corner to the right, and there in front was the panorama again, closer and emptier and clear all the way to the deck of the *San Andreas*.

Except for Francis.

He had just reached the pier after completing his false-alarm task and was starting up one of the planks onto the ship. Gabe and Vangie and Roscoe and Ittzy all bawled at him at once to get out of the way, and their combined racket made him turn and look over his shoulder.

Here came the gold wagon, crossing the flats at the bottom of the hill, barreling this way with undiminished speed.

Ruffled for once in his life, Francis legged it up the plank. Behind him he could hear the booming thunder of the wagon as it shot out from the end of the street onto the wooden pier. The thunder was coming closer incredibly fast.

Francis dashed for the deck. The plank suddenly rumbled beneath his feet. He didn't look behind him, because he *knew* something was gaining on him; it was on the plank with him.

He dove from the plank, sideways toward the deck, trying to land on the relative softness of a coil of rope. The wagon flashed up the planks past the spot where he'd just been, thudded to the deck with a bone-rattling jar, careened across the ship and crashed to a shuddering stop against the pile of hay bales stacked up against the base of the mainmast.

There was a second of stunned silence, everywhere in the world. Francis sat up on the coil of rope and blinked. Then, like a lazy railroad semaphore, the mast tilted slowly and fell across the wagon, just behind Ittzy and just in front of Gabe, landing with a crackling, grinding roar and disintegrating itself into kindling.

Gabe looked at it. He seemed to be deaf. "Uh," he said.

26

As the last echoes of the self-destructing mast faded into history, Captain Flagway emerged from his cabin and walked forward toward the gold wagon as though the deck were heaving under his feet in a heavy storm. An almost empty whisky bottle was clutched in his right hand.

Roscoe's crew was swarming over the ship, casting off lines, raising sail, shouting nautical gutterances at one another. Ittzy and Roscoe were stretching a tarpaulin over the length of the gold wagon. Vangie was seated on a water barrel, fixing her hair with the aid of an ivory comb and a small mirror. Francis was brushing hemp flecks from the seat of his trousers. Gabe was standing by the side rail, tensely watching an endless stream of mounted men pouring from the main gate of the Mint, thundering downhill toward the pier.

And up in the rigging, there was no wind.

Gabe collared Roscoe. "Why the hell aren't we moving? They're after us!"

Roscoe looked up, shielded his eyes with his hand, and studied the sails. "No wind," he decided.

Everybody else also looked up. Captain Flagway, in looking

up, overbalanced himself and sat down on the deck. He went on looking up.

"I don't believe it," Gabe said. The posse was topping the nearer slope, men and riders leaping down the second hill. "I just don't believe it," he said.

Vangie closed her eyes, the mirror and comb forgotten in her lap. Now that disaster had struck, she was no longer loud. "I knew it," she said quietly. "I knew it, I knew it all along."

Gabe tottered across the deck, staring upward. He still couldn't believe it.

The Bay was filled with ship traffic, and a steamer, *Daniel Webster*, was sliding past just now, outward bound for the Golden Gate. It passed very close to the *San Andreas* and its wake made the water heave, causing the *San Andreas* to roll from side to side on the ripples.

The motion took Gabe's mind away from the empty sails. Greenly he staggered back and turned to the rail. Leaning there, he watched the steamship easing by just a few feet away, nearly close enough to touch.

Gabe stared at that other ship. Why couldn't the *San Andreas* move like that? He looked upward and saw no sails on *Daniel Webster*, only a black stack spouting smoke. And that was the difference right there—the difference between being old-fashioned and out of date and caught, or being modern and up to date and safe.

Then the thought hit him. "God *damn*," he whispered, just for himself, and suddenly forgot about being sick or caught or any of that negative stuff. "I've got it!" he yelled, and smacked the rail with his palm.

The rest of them had been alternately watching the posse getting closer and the sails staying empty. Now they turned and watched Gabe suddenly race across the littered deck toward the prow of the ship. Just beyond him, *Daniel Webster* steamed majestically along, matching his pace, so that to the rest it looked as though Gabe and the steamship were fixed in one spot while the *San Andreas* was sliding backward.

Captain Flagway covered one eye, the better to see and comprehend what was happening. Unfortunately, he then closed the uncovered eye instead of the covered one and could see nothing at all. "An eclipse," he suggested. "They'll never find us in the dark."

Ashore, the posse thundered to the bottom of the hill and streamed toward the pier.

Aboard, Roscoe's crew huddled together, trying to look like a passing acrobat act that had nothing to do with all this. Ittzy was calmly lashing the tarp over the gold. Roscoe and Francis, side by side, stared at the oncoming posse. Captain Flagway tried to see in the dark. Vangie was tearing her hair.

Gabe reached the bow and lunged to the rusty anchor that lay on the deck. He picked it up with a great rattle of chains, and with superhuman effort heaved it out across the rippling water.

The stern of the steamer was just passing, and the flying anchor fell across her taffrail like a grappling hook.

The posse hit the pier like Bedford Forrest's cavalry. You could count every tooth in every horse's mouth.

Daniel Webster steamed ponderously on into the fog **and** the anchor chain ran out from its rusty winch, making a sagging dip into the water between the two ships until suddenly the winch caught, the U-shaped sag became shallower, the dripping rusty links lifted out of the water, the chain became a straight line, the straight line because taut—and the *San Andreas* was all but jerked from the water.

She leaped away from the pier and went churning off in the wake of *Daniel Webster*, heading straight for a passing fogbank, pulling out from the pier just as the lead horsemen were starting up the planks. The planks slid along the pier, angling to keep one end on the ship and one on the pier, held down by the weight of horses and riders, until the *San Andreas* moved out from shore, turning away from San Francisco and toward wherever *Daniel Webster* had it in mind to go.

The planks couldn't stretch. They lost their grip, the outer edges slid off the rail of the ship, and planks and horses and horsemen and all went bubbling and screaming and flailing their way into the water. Men sat on horses who stood on planks that fell rapidly through the air and slapped mightily at the ocean, sinking everybody.

And that's how the surfboard was invented.

Out in the Bay the great white fogbank bounced lazily, like God's beachball. The two ships steamed steadily toward it.

Seven horsemen in the posse didn't stop in time and followed the leaders into the water. The rest milled around on the pier getting things sorted out. One or two of them started shooting at the disappearing ship, and then they all opened up with a fusillade of gunfire over which their angry voices roared with frustration and rage.

Into the fog steamed *Daniel Webster*, unwittingly towing a decrepit sailing ship with her sails filling in the wrong direction.

The red-haired cop, McCorkle, raced onto the dock with his huge notebook brandished in the air. "Halt! Pull over to the pier!"

Bullets punched holes in the rotten wood of the *San Andreas* at the waterline and below decks thin little fountains began to arc into the bilges.

Roscoe's crew swarmed aloft to furl the sails before they braked *Daniel Webster* to a stop. And meanwhile on board the steamship, the captain was studying his gauges in a state of confusion bordering on apoplexy. He turned to the speaking tube and yelled down to the engine room: "More speed, damn it! What's wrong with you down there?"

"Captain, she's goin' full out. Whaddya want from us?"

"We're only making five bloody knots, and how are we supposed to beat the bloody clipper record that way?" The captain straightened up and looked around into the thickening fog, trying to figure out why his ship had slowed down.

Aboard the *San Andreas*, joy was unrestrained. Vangie, in relief and elation, allowed herself to be kissed by Francis and Ittzy and Captain Flagway (who had found his sight and his legs again in the general triumph). Then Roscoe and his crew approached, wiping their mouths on their sleeves, and Vangie switched to shaking hands.

They were in the fog now. Francis peered around in its cottony whiteness, saying, "Where's Gabe? The man's brilliant, he should be toasted in champagne. Where is he?"

"He was here a minute ago," Ittzy said.

"Maybe he went ashore during the eclipse," Captain Flagway suggested.

Vangie looked all around. "Gabe? Gabe?"

They found him at last hanging over the rail. "No champagne," he groaned. "For God's sake, no champagne."

27

"Fog's thinning out," Captain Flagway said. He was watching the taut anchor chain that extended into the fog ahead of them. He was beginning to make out the shape of the steamship just ahead.

Somewhere in the vague foggy distance behind them there were bells and sirens and gunshot-signals. It was all unhappily reminiscent of various chases and battles Flagway had drunk his way through along the South American coast. Here he was in motion for the first time in three years, on the deck of a ship slicing through the water, and he hated it.

Flagway hated the sea. He always had. All he wanted was a railroad ticket to Baltimore.

It was definitely lifting. The fog. He saw the vague shape of a man striding into the stern of the steamer.

That must be the captain, he thought. He almost waved to the man. After all they were colleagues.

Yes, it was definitely the steamer's captain. You could tell by the way he started screaming, shaking his fist, and throwing his gold-braided hat on the deck and jumping up and down on it.

Finally the fellow went away for a few minutes. When he returned he had two sailors with him, and they both carried crowbars. They started prying at the anchor hooked into their stern rail.

All at once the steamship leaped forward, the anchor flew into the air, and the captain and two sailors and two crowbars all fell *bloop* into a scrambling mass of arms and legs.

And *Daniel Webster* steamed off into the mist, quickly absorbing herself from view.

He smelled Roscoe's approach. "Got a little breeze up out here," Roscoe said. "I'll get the boys to run up the canvas. You want to go steer?"

Flagway edged away from him. "Why shur—shut—shertainly."

"Due north after we bust out the Golden Gate. That's where m'brother's got the other ship."

On the way to the tiller Flagway noticed Gabe, still draped over the rail like a suit waiting to be sent to the cleaner's.

Beyond Gabe he noticed the gold wagon again. Well after all it was only the Government's money. Governments did all sorts of things with money, but Flagway couldn't think of any government that had ever done him any good personally. All he really wanted out of life was to get home and go back to helping Daddy in the apothecary shop. Was that so much to ask? Yet the governments of sixteen countries had prevented him from achieving that simple goal for more years than he could count.

Manning the tiller and peering glazedly into the thinning mist, Captain Flagway watched Roscoe's toughs swarm up into the rigging and loose the sails to the wind. He aimed the lumbering ship north into the Pacific Ocean.

28

Slowly, Gabe lifted his head.
The horizon was doing seesaw
things.

Vangie said, "Feeling any better?"

"I'm either cured or dead. I think."

"You mean it's all over?"

"I mean, I think the teething ring I lost when I was eight months old has just turned up."

Weakly he turned around and leaned his back against the rail to survey the ship. Roscoe was marching about giving orders to his crew in a voice like a bassoon. Captain Flagway was at the tiller making drunken gestures, flanked by Francis and Ittzy. The gold wagon crouched under its tarp with the broken mainmast across it.

"We made it," Gabe said slowly. "How about that. We made it."

"So far," Vangie said.

"Boy, you are something," he said. "You are really something. You just never give up. Now just what the hell do you mean, 'so far'?"

"We're in the middle of the ocean. So what happens when

we land again? Don't you think the police will be waiting to arrest you?"

"No."

"Well, you're probably right about that. Because we'll never get that far. Roscoe and his brother will probably feed us to the fishes first."

"I'm glad the sea air makes you so cheerful."

"When Roscoe throws your dead body overboard, don't say I didn't warn you."

"I probably won't say a word."

"And there's another thing. Isn't the ship wallowing kind of low in the water?"

He shrugged. "Probably the gold."

"We'll never get away with it," she said. "Not in a million years."

"Yeah."

"Did you see the headline in that paper last week when they hanged those murderers? JERKED TO JESUS. That's what they're going to do to us."

He closed her in the circle of his arms. "Yeah."

"Don't think you're going to shut me up by romancing me, Gabe Beauchamps." Then she gave a strangled little cry and stiffened in his arms.

Gabe leaned back a bit to look at her and saw her staring forward. He turned his head, and here came Roscoe and his crew, fanned out across the deck, a little less menacing than the armies of Attila the Hun.

Roscoe was armed with his two enormous pistols, and his men brandished huge knives and belaying pins.

Gabe knew the answer to the question, but he asked it anyway: "What's up, Roscoe?"

"Your time, buster," Roscoe said. He gestured with the guns. "We're taking over."

Vangie, anger and frustration in her voice, said, "I *told* you!"

"Easy," Gabe told her.

Francis, coming up next to Gabe, frowned at the tough guys and said, "Roscoe, whatever is the meaning of this?"

For once, Roscoe had no trouble meeting Francis' eye. "It means you're sharkbait, pretty boy," he said. "You and all the rest of them."

Out of the corner of his eye, Gabe saw Vangie drifting away to the right. Did she have something in mind, or was she just moving aimlessly, out of fear? To keep Roscoe's attention, just in case there was something afoot in Vangie's agile brain, Gabe said, "You can't run things without me, Roscoe, you ought to know that."

Roscoe grinned, sure of himself. "You don't think so, huh?"

"Not a chance," Gabe said, and made himself grin just as easily and self-confidently as Roscoe. "You couldn't find your nose with your hand if you didn't have help."

Roscoe's grin faded. The pistols in his hands leveled themselves more specifically at Gabe. His voice grating with meanness, Roscoe said, "You talk pretty tough, New York boy. But I'm the one with the guns in my hands."

"Oh, Roscoe," Francis said. "Do stop playing at being a big boy."

"We'll see about that," Roscoe said. "You people just move yourselves over by that rail there."

Francis was looking pale but clearly determined not to show any fear. "Why?" he asked.

"We're about to find out," Roscoe said, "just how good you folks can swim."

"Listen," Gabe said, but he never got to finish the sentence, because all at once Vangie made her play.

The movement was just a blur; her years of pocket-picking experience came in very handy when it was her own pocket she was picking. Out came Gabe's knuckle-duster, moving so fast he could hardly make out himself what she had in her hand, and she fired the one bullet it contained.

It was either a brilliant shot or a lucky one. It knocked one of Roscoe's guns right out of his hand.

Gabe whipped the whisky flask from his hip pocket and leveled it at Roscoe. "Drop it, Roscoe," he said, "and don't make a move."

Roscoe was already bending over his numbed hand. Now he dropped his second gun and clutched at his injury.

His crew started to move forward, raising their clubs and knives, closing in on Gabe and Vangie and Francis, with Captain Flagway at the wheel just behind them.

"No!" Roscoe cried, waving his men back with his good hand. "That thing's a——"

"——gun," Gabe finished, and fired one shot into the air. The crew hesitated.

Francis grabbed a handy marlin spike, and pointed it at the tough guys. "Yes," he said. "And this is a gun."

Ittzy took the explosives book from his pocket. "And *this* is a gun."

Captain Flagway unscrewed a spoke from the wheel and brandished it, not too steadily. "Yes, and *thish* is a gun," he said.

The tough guys looked at one another, at Roscoe, and at the array of objects being pointed at them. More bewildered than anything else, they dropped their arsenal of weapons and raised their hands into the air.

"That's smart," Gabe told them. "Francis, get around behind and disarm them."

"That'll be a pleasure," Francis said.

"Then we'll tie them up and stow them below."

Roscoe snarled. "Okay, okay," he said. "But you wait'll my brother gets his hands on you."

29

In the Pacific Ocean just outside the Golden Gate two San Francisco Police launches sliced through the water toward a distant fast-moving smudge of smoke. In the bow of the leading launch stood McCorkle, shading his eyes to scan the horizons. He pointed toward the smoke and the launches picked up speed to go charging after it. McCorkle took out his notebook and made a note.

Elsewhere in the Pacific, Francis stood in the bow of the *San Andreas* and pointed toward a distant motionless smudge of smoke. "That's probably the *Sea Wolf*."

Gabe said, "Okay, everybody knows what to do."

"Get killed," Vangie said.

Down in the hold Roscoe and his gang sat roped and gagged on the floor. Water was starting to slosh around on the floorboards.

Roscoe grunted. His eyes went wide with alarm as he watched the water run across the decking. He began to thump his heels on the boards. The rest of the gang followed suit, and they got a pretty good drum chorus going, accompanied by strangled grunts. But it didn't seem to be doing any good. There was no sign anyone up on deck could hear them.

Miles to the south, the police launches closed slowly with the fast-moving smudge of smoke.

The motionless smudge of smoke to the north was coming into view of the *San Andreas*, close enough now to reveal the ship beneath it: *Sea Wolf*—rough, scaly, rusty, dark, grim, ominous.

Vangie, watching it loom ahead of them, closed her eyes and leaned faintly against the foremast, shaking her head dismally.

Slowly the two ships converged.

Captain Flagway uttered slurred suggestions having to do with the placement of ropelines. Francis and Ittzy waited by the rails while Flagway guided the ship, lurching and heeling, into a position approximately broadside to *Sea Wolf*. Lines flew across to lash the ships together.

Gabe had reloaded everything that passed for a gun and distributed them all among his crew. He stood now with one of Roscoe's huge revolers in his belt and watched cautiously while mangy-looking sailors moved forward to *Sea Wolf's* rusty rail and tossed several planks across to make a bridge between the two ships' decks.

There was a moment of silence, then, when nothing at all happened. Gabe could feel the tension in his own unlikely crew; Francis trying to look mean, Vangie trying to look tough, Captain Flagway trying to look sober, and Ittzy——

Gabe glanced around. Ittzy was just sort of standing there, unconcerned. Gabe wondered how the little man would get out of this one, and whether or not any of the rest of them would ride out of it all on his coattails.

There was somebody coming. Gabe faced *Sea Wolf* again.

A heavy-set gent with an eyepatch and a hook for a hand had appeared. A marlin spike was stuck in the thick rope holding up his trousers, and what looked like a rope burn circled his neck. He came thumping across to the *San Andreas* on one of the planks, jumped down onto the deck, and stood glaring around, sizing everybody up.

"He *is* meaner-looking than Roscoe," Vangie whispered.

Captain Flagway sighed. "I wish I was in Baltimore."

The big man with the eyepatch and the hook and the marlin spike gradually narrowed in on Gabe, fixed him with his eye, and said, "Where's Roscoe?"

Gabe moved forward, mostly because he so much wanted to move back. "Roscoe's below," he said. "You his brother?"

"Me?" Chuckling, the big man shook his head and said, "I ain't that tough. I'm First Mate Crung."

Gabe said, "Well, where's Percival?"

"You shouldn't call him that," First Mate Crung said softly. "He mought hear you. Captain Arafoot is who he prefers to be."

"Well, where is he?"

"Captain Arafoot never leaves his cabin at sea."

Gabe started to grin. "Seasick, huh."

"Naw. It's just that every time he comes out he kills two or three guys, and we can't afford to lose crew that fast."

Vangie uttered a faint moan.

Well, it was no time to turn back. And the *San Andreas* had gone just about as far as she could. She was settling in the water—even a landlubber could see that much. Gabe said bleakly, "Well, I'll go over to him then. Meanwhile why don't you get your crew to start moving that wagon over to your ship? We're a little short-handed over here."

Crung frowned around at the deck. Ittzy, Francis, Flagway, Gabe, Vangie. Nobody else around. "So I see."

Vangie grabbed Gabe's sleeve. "Don't go."

"Vangie, when you're caught in a rising flood you don't just sit down and pray for drought. I got to." And he stepped past Crung, walked across the planks onto the rusty deck of the steamship, and stepped aside to let the half-dozen crewmen past who'd been summoned by Crung. They were a slinking, cowering lot, scurrying across and ducking away from him and from everybody else who stood upright. Something, he judged, had scared the guts out of all of them.

It wasn't hard to guess what it was.

Vangie watched Gabe walk on board *Sea Wolf* as if it were a tightrope. She wanted to cry. It was such a shame. So much ingenuity and courage, devoted to a doomed mission.

She watched Gabe climb across coiled hawsers and reach the door of the captain's cabin. He knocked briskly and waited.

Even from here she could hear the sudden *roar* that boomed from the cabin. She shrank back and felt herself wanting to cower just like Captain Arafoot's crew.

Gabe pulled the door open and strode into the cabin. She watched with one eye. He'd left the door ajar behind him, but she couldn't see into the darkness within.

The *roar* increased to a ROAR.

Meanwhile, the Arafoot crew pushed and shoved, sweating and whining. They were trying to maneuver the gold wagon toward the planks that bridged the two ships, but the wagon weighed close to three tons and wasn't very helpful. When they finally got it away from the stack of hay bales, it began to roll in the wrong direction—toward the windward rail.

Ittzy leaped onto the wagon and grabbed the brake handle.

After that Ittzy stayed on top of the wagon to steer with the wagon-tongue and stay close to the brake. The crewmen hustled and groaned and heaved and sweated, and slowly the wagon moved toward the planks.

Vangie saw the activity out of the corner of her eye while she watched the dark doorway of Captain Percival Arafoot's cabin. Her hand was to her mouth. What could be going on in there?

Suddenly Gabe came pelting backwards out of the cabin as if he'd been nudged in the chest by a railroad engine doing ninety miles an hour. He tumbled head over heels across the deck.

But at once he scrambled back to his feet, rushed to the cabin door, slammed it shut and jammed a bar down across it.

It didn't make the ROAR recede to a *roar*. It remained a ROAR, growing louder if anything. The door began to rattle and shake against the bar.

Vangie saw Gabe brush sweat from his brow and lean shaking against a rusty ventilator hood.

The gold wagon was up on the planks now, with *Sea Wolf's* crew cringing under Crung's shouts, trying to manhandle it across to their ship.

But the two vessels were riding up and down on the water, not in unison, and the planks kept tilting back and forth, so that the wagon rolled forward and back, forward and back, never quite making it all the way to the deck of either ship and never quite falling into the sea between them.

Vangie saw Gabe react to the sight of all that gold out there swinging precariously above the frothy sea. His face filled with pale alarm; he moved forward with arms outstretched, calling something. It was as if he wanted to gather the wagon into his arms and bring it gently and safely to the deck of *Sea Wolf* all by himself through sheer strength of will.

And then the tilt of the ships sharpened. The wagon

careened forward onto *Sea Wolf*'s deck, scattering sailors like birdshot.

The wagon made a sweeping curve around the deck with Ittzy steering madly on top. It teetered near the far rail, and Gabe was running after it like a crazed jilted lover, waving his hands in the air. It began to topple over the side. Gabe jumped up and down, yelling.

The sea lifted. *Sea Wolf* rolled a few degrees. The wagon was returned to the deck by that motion; it kept on moving, and Vangie suddenly realized it was juggernauting directly toward Captain Arafoot's cabin. With Gabe still in hot pursuit.

The wagon swept past a tangle of ropes and barreled with a tremendous crash into the cabin.

It demolished the outer wall. Dense dust and debris flew in all directions. Everybody stopped to stare.

In the sudden silence the ROAR climbed to a ROAR that vibrated through both ships, shaking them to their keels.

Vangie blinked. She tried to stare through the pall of dust and flying objects. What was happening?

From the cloud emerged a giant figure draped in the tarp that had been covering the gold.

The tarp walked on legs. It was tied around with ropes, and with every ROAR, it shimmered and vibrated like the asbestos curtain at the finale of a cancan show.

Behind the canvas-wrapped giant there emerged from the dust a sword. After the sword came Ittzy.

The point of the sword was lightly prodding the rear of the ROAR.

As the two figures progressed out of the cloud, Gabe stepped in front of the ROAR, stopped it with a hand in the middle of the canvas, then bopped it on the top with a belaying pin.

The ROAR modulated through ROAR to *roar* to roar to a kind of clogged silence. The tarped figure swayed on its feet.

Gabe yelled across to the *San Andreas*: "Crung. Hey Crung!"

"Yeah?"

"Get all your crew over there with you on Captain Flagway's ship. Every man-jack."

"Yeah? What for?"

"Just do what I say."

Crung walked out onto the planks between the ships and stood there steady as a rock. Vangie shuddered. Crung said softly, with menace, "And if I don't?"

"Maybe," Gabe told him, "I'll release Captain Arafoot here and let you explain to him why you wouldn't obey orders when I was holding him hostage. Or maybe I'll just throw him over the side and feed him to the sharks. I haven't quite made up my mind yet."

Crung nodded thoughtfully. It wasn't that he was giving in. It was just that he was thinking, and with Crung that was obviously a slow process.

His one eye blinked. His one hand toyed with the marlin spike. He turned slowly and surveyed the deck of *San Andreas*. His eye flicked from Francis to Vangie to Captain Flagway. "Well now," he said slowly, "if it don't look like I've got me some hostages, too. How about that now?"

Vangie whipped out the knuckle-duster. "Forget it, buster."

Captain Flagway staggered out from the tiller, braced his feet and addressed himself to Crung. "Now, look here. I'm a peash—peaceloving man. I have never disemboweled anyone in my life. I'm a bit long in the tooth to start gouching—gouging men's eyes out and chopping their heads off, and crashing—cracking their skulls with clubs. I just don't think I could stand to do things like that."

"Yeah?"

"So I wish you would just pay attention to what Mr. Beauchampsh tells you, and do what he says, and not make any fuss.'"

Crung blinked at Captain Flagway. He blinked at the knuckle-duster wavering in Vangie's hand. He turned his head and blinked at Ittzy and the sword. He blinked at Gabe, and saw him holding the flask. In a tone of exasperated despair, he cried, "And what's *that* supposed to be?"

"It's supposed to be a flask," Gabe said, and fired a shot in the air. "But it's a gun."

Crung turned his head back and forth, looking from one of them to another. "You're all crazy people," he said. "All of you. All except that fruity-looking one there."

Francis stiffened. "Anyone who dresses himself in that overmasculine way," he said coolly, "and chooses to spend utterly *months* at a time at sea without women, nothing but men for companionship, is *hardly* in any position to cast aspersions. I've met a goodly number of you sailor types, believe you me, and if there's one thing I've learned it's that——"

"Arright! Ar*right!*" Crung turned very quickly toward *Sea Wolf* and bellowed: "All hands!"

"Fruity indeed," Francis said.

Vangie said, "Never mind, Francis, just consider the source."

"Oh, I do."

"Get over here onto this miserable hulk," Crung yelled at his crew, and at once they slunk and slouched across onto the *San Andreas*, never meeting anyone's eyes.

After the *Sea Wolf* had been emptied of all its original personnel except for Captain Percival Arafoot, Gabe cried, "Vangie, come on over! Francis, Captain Flagway!"

Vangie had been propping the knuckle-duster on the tiller. "Francis," she said, "would you mind terribly holding this for me?"

"Oh, my dear, of course not. How remiss of me. Here, I'll carry it."

The knuckle-duster looked, if anything, less appropriate in Francis' hand than in Vangie's; still, he wore it with a certain dash.

The three of them skirted the muttering crew and crossed the planks to *Sea Wolf*. Midway, Vangie looked down at the water heaving between the two ships and for the first time truly understood Gabe's reaction to the sea. But she forced herself to keep moving, following the weaving, perilous Captain Flagway, and once aboard the solid *Sea Wolf*, she felt better again.

"Okay, Percival," Gabe said. "Time for you to walk the plank."

"ROAR."

"Move, now," Gabe insisted. "You can take your teeth with you, or you can leave them behind. Which is it?"

"*Roar*."

Ittzy pricked the tarp with the point of his sword, and the tarp-wrapped figure felt its way out onto the planks, guiding on the sound of Crung's voice: "Keep that son of a bitch off here, damn it! He'll kill all of us. Can't you have a little goddamn decency and shove him overboard?"

Ittzy and Francis were fumbling with knots in the ropes that held the two ships together. Captain Flagway was making his way to the controls on the bridge.

The ships began to draw apart. Gabe said, "Hey Crung."

"Yeah?"

"Keep him tied up, he won't do any damage."

"You don't know him."

"Well, he's your problem now, I guess. But you've got some help. You'll find Roscoe and his gang down below in the hold. And listen—one more thing. The olivers are looking for that ship you're on. You better move on out of here fast. I'd head north along the coast if I were you."

Vangie saw the look of satisfaction on Gabe's face as he turned away. She felt proud and sad, both at once: all that brilliance in a doomed enterprise.

He said, "Well, what do you think now? Are we going to get away with it?"

"Not in a million years." She smiled sadly, fondly. "But nobody else could have come as close."

30

Out in another part of the ocean the two police launches closed in on *Daniel Webster*. It took several minutes—and one shot across the steamer's bow—to convince the captain to slow down and listen, and then he did nothing for a while but bellow unintelligibly through a megaphone. Eventually he became calm enough to hear the questions they were asking; then he gestured violently northward, losing his megaphone over the side in the process.

The two launches veered around and went charging away to the north. The captain of *Daniel Webster* flung his hat after his megaphone, screamed at heaven, and went raging back to the bridge to kick his helmsman.

Farther north, the *Sea Wolf* was traveling south. Below, in the heat and noise and semidarkness of the bowels of the ship, Gabe was working as coal handler. Stripped to the waist, he was shoveling coal from the bin into the wheelbarrow, pushing it laboriously through the narrow corridor to the engine room—risking his knuckles along the metal

walls every time—and dumping it on the small sooty pile behind Ittzy.

Ittzy was the stoker, shoveling coal into the furnace. Sweaty,
dirty, also stripped to the waist, gasping for breath, Ittzy
turned a broadly smiling face toward Gabe and yelled over
the roar of the engine, "This is fun!"

Gabe looked at him. He panted, but had nothing to say.

"Well," Ittzy yelled, a bit less exuberantly, "it's anyway
better than being locked in that back room."

Gabe turned and plodded away with his wheelbarrow.

Up on the bridge Captain Flagway was steering. The coast
was to his left, San Francisco was just beyond the horizon to
the south, and Baltimore was not very far beyond that. Baltimore; Daddy; the apothecary shop. After all these years.

Sea Wolf was a lean, fast, hungry ship—a pleasure to
operate. Captain Flagway, for the first time he could remember, smiled.

On deck, Vangie frowned, and paused in her labors. She
and Francis were packing gold ingots into small wooden
boxes marked TEAK. Once all the gold was packed away,
the wagon would be broken up and dumped over the side.

Still frowning, pensively gazing toward the horizon, Vangie
said, "Francis?"

"Mm?"

"I want you to know," she said, "that I like you very much."

"Well, thank you," he said, surprised.

She looked at him, a sad smile touching her lips. "Very
soon now," she said, "we're all going to be arrested and put
away forever in separate prisons, but I do want you to know
I've grown very fond of you."

Touched, Francis said, "You've been a sister to me,
Vangie."

"And you to me."

"But maybe we *won't* be caught," he said. "We've gotten away with it so far."

Vangie sighed. "Maybe you're right," she said, without conviction.

Farther north, aboard the *San Andreas,* First Mate Crung was untying Roscoe in the knee-deep water in the hold, while other crewmen were doing the same for Roscoe's companions. From above, a steady malevolent ROAR could be heard.

Roscoe, free of his gag, looked up and said, "Percy's all right, eh?"

"He's a little annoyed. I figured I'd better keep him tied up a while."

"Not a bad idea," Roscoe said. Rubbing his wrists where the rope had chafed them, he looked around at the water lapping everywhere. "This damn tub's sinking," he said. "We better get to the lifeboats."

Gabe was taking a breather on deck, his place below being temporarily taken by Francis, who had insisted on finding out how real sailors live.

Gabe and Vangie leaned against the rail, their arms around one another. Neither had much to say; Gabe out of weariness, Vangie out of pessimism.

Captain Flagway called from the bridge, "Ships ahead. Coming this way."

Gabe watched them, idly interested. "In a hurry," he said.

Vangie suddenly clutched his arm. "Police."

"Take it easy," he told her. "They're not looking for this ship. It's the *San Andreas* they want. That was the whole idea of the switch."

Nevertheless, he could feel how tense she was as the two police launches arrived and shot past to starboard, thundering northward. Standing up in the bow of the lead launch was a red-haired figure, straining forward. McCorkle.

Gabe frowned, watching that shock of red hair go by. "Is that bluebottle everywhere?"

"That's what I've been trying to tell you," Vangie said. "*Some* bluebottle is everywhere. You just can't get away, Gabe."

He looked at her, trying to keep his confidence. Rational problems he could work out, but superstitions were harder to deal with. Could she be right after all?

Then, from the bridge, Captain Flagway sang out, "There it is! San Francisco, dead ahead!"

Gabe laughed, in sudden relief. "They're not everywhere," he said, and looked out toward the distant hills of the city.

The police launches very nearly missed the *San Andreas* entirely. All that was left of her when they arrived was the gently descending top six feet of her foremast, with the Paraguayan flag fluttering in the breeze, as though somewhere beneath the surface of the water someone was holding a garden party.

Officer McCorkle, in the prow of the lead launch, removed his hat and held it over his heart. His red hair flew and flickered in the breeze, like an answer to the Paraguayan flag.

The two launches circled the sinking ship. The mast settled slowly, as bubbles popped to the surface here and there. The flag dipped, wetted itself, wrapped itself dankly around the mast, and disappeared at last into the sea.

Officer McCorkle replaced his hat. Then he took out his notebook, flipped through it, studied an entry here and there, shook his head, and tossed the notebook into the ocean.

31

Up the dusty slope toward Francis's gold mine came a large wagon full of small boxes marked TEAK. Ittzy was driving, and Gabe was sitting on the high seat beside him, smiling around at the countryside. Captain Flagway was perched atop the cargo with his braided cap at a jaunty angle and half-full flask of whisky dangling from his hand. Francis and Vangie rode a brace of matched white horses beside the wagon.

The sun shone. Birds sang. An occasional rabbit hoppity-hopped across the green and sunny landscape.

They arrived at the entrance to the mine, and all dismounted. Francis said, "I can't help it, you know, I just have trouble *absorbing* this. We're bringing gold to a gold mine."

"That's right," Gabe said. "And we're going to start selling it right back to the Mint again, one bar at a time." He turned to give Vangie a big grin and say, "Unless you still think we're gonna get caught."

She looked all around in the sunlight, frowning and squinting as though baffled by the nonappearance of the United

States cavalry. "I just can't understand it," she said. "How can the Government let a thing like this happen?"

"I guess they must be thinking about something else today," Gabe said.

Captain Flagway leaned against the wagon and toasted the world at large with his flask. A crumpled smile was on his lips and a sputtering gleam in his eye. "Oh, happy day," he announced. "At last I'll be going back to Balsi—Balder—Baltimore!"

Gabe grinned at him. "That's right, Captain," he said. "You're on your way."

"*Well* on my way."

Vangie, trying not to show her emotions on the surface, said, "Well, Gabe, I guess you'll be on your way, too. Back to New York."

"New York." Gabe smiled faintly in reminiscence, then frowned a bit, gazing out over the hills toward San Francisco. Wisps of fog were beginning to drift through the valleys with the approach of sunset. "Old Twill," Gabe said, thoughtfully. "You know what the trouble with Twill is?"

Vangie didn't care what the trouble with Twill was. She wanted to know what the trouble was with Gabe Beauchamps. "No, I don't," she said.

"He doesn't understand where the future is. Life is moving West, Vangie. This is where the future is—right out here."

She couldn't believe her ears. "Do you mean that, Gabe?"

"I'm kind of getting used to things out here," he said.

"You are?"

"The slower pace, the smalltown life." He shrugged. "San Francisco isn't too bad, for a yokelville."

Francis said delightedly, "Gabe, you mean you'll stay?"

"The burg has possibilities," Gabe said. "I might invest here."

"The cancan shows," Francis said. "They're going to open again, I got inside word. You could——"

"No," Gabe said thoughtfully, "I don't think so."

"Oh, yes, Gabe!" Vangie cried. "Show business!"

"The cancan shows," Francis said, "are the wave of the future. A man could get in right now on the ground floor. That's what I'm doing with my share, becoming an entrepreneur."

Vangie clutched Gabe's arm. "Oh, Gabe, say yes!"

"I just don't think so," Gabe said.

Vangie frowned at him, bewildered again. "Well, what, then?"

"I've been thinking," Gabe said, "about real estate."

"Real estate?" Vangie looked around, looked back at Gabe again. "You mean houses?"

"No, land."

"But all the land in San Francisco is already built on."

"Outside town," Gabe said. He nodded, agreeing with himself. "Across the Bay, I think."

"Across the *Bay*?"

"Land should be cheap over there."

Vangie said, "Well, of *course* it's cheap. There's no way to get to it, nobody wants it."

"Some day," Gabe said, "there'll be a bridge across the Golden Gate."

Vangie stamped her foot in impatience and disbelief. "For Heaven's sake, there will not!"

Francis said, "I do doubt that, Gabe, you know. That's far too wide for any bridge."

"I think they'll do it anyway," Gabe said. "Put a bridge right across. And then that land up there . . . What's it called, anyway?"

"Oh, who knows!" Vangie cried.

"Marin County," Francis said. "But Vangie's right, Gabe,

that land up there won't be worth much. Now, the cancan shows——"

"No," Gabe said. He just had a feeling deep down inside that he was right. "Land," he said.

"I'm going to open a chain of discount stores," Ittzy said. "And never clerk in any of them."

"I'll stick to land," Gabe said.

"Oh, Gabe," Vangie cried, at her wit's end. "You've done everything right, you got away with the robbery even though you shouldn't, and now you're just going to throw it all away."

"Land," Gabe said.

"You never listen!"

Gabe nodded. "That's right," he said.

He gazed out over the raw new countryside; his countryside now. Vangie and Francis talked to him, argued with him, pleaded with him—but he never listened.

ABOUT THE AUTHORS

BRIAN GARFIELD lives in the pre-1900 general store of Alpine, New Jersey with his wife, English actress Shan Willson, and a platoon of dogs and cats. The thirty-four year old Arizonan has been a jazz musician, a college instructor, and a reluctant soldier. He has lived in many places from San Francisco to Paris, and has written several well-received novels ranging in subject matter from Wall Street to the Old West. Described by the New York *Times* as a "virtuoso," he is the author of the non-fiction study *The Thousand Mile War*, as well as the recent suspense thriller *Death Wish* which has become a "cult" book and will soon appear as a United Artists film. A former president of the Western Writers of America, Mr. Garfield reports that shortly before writing his half of GANGWAY he was caught cheating at cards and was shot by Donald E. Westlake with a .32-caliber poker chip.

ABOUT THE AUTHORS

DONALD E. WESTLAKE was born in a filling station near Aardvark, Oklahoma, early in February. Attending public schools in Pittsburgh, Akron, and Sinking Province, he took his degree in elliptical engineering from the Brooklyn Academy of Music late in June. Mr. Westlake has operated a bootleg yellow pages factory in Detroit, panned for gold in Albania, and was the copywriter responsible for the unintentional double meaning in the Prune Whip Yogurt advertising campaign of 1966-67. Turning to writing after his left leg was bitten by an alligator in the New York City sewer system, Mr. Westlake has addressed himself to the central concerns of our troubled times with all the verse and passion with which he pursued his earlier, more active career. His first novel, *Sprigs of Eiderdown,* won the coveted *Prix Fixe,* the most prestigious literary award ever offered by the city of Marseilles. Many of his tales of adventure have been made into television playlets without his knowledge or consent. He makes his home in a converted bathysphere in Lake Como, Switzerland, and has never paid any income tax.